# *WHAT WAS THAT SMELL?*

Suddenly every muscle in my body sprang tight and taut. In my mind's eye I could see the old medicine man who told fortunes at the Fourth of July sideshow, back in Abilene.

*"You will see yourself in the eye of the great bear,"* he had said.

I saw myself standing near the cage where the old black bear was. Waiting with the crowd of people. Hoping he would open his eyes so I could see myself.

That was the smell!

It was a . . .

"BEAR!"

I screamed the word at the top of my lungs. I grabbed for Mama's arm.

It was too late. Daddy had already disappeared inside the cabin.

**Books by Bill Wallace**

Red Dog
Trapped in Death Cave

Available from ARCHWAY Paperbacks

Aloha Summer
The Backward Bird Dog
Beauty
The Biggest Klutz in Fifth Grade
Blackwater Swamp
Buffalo Gal
The Christmas Spurs
Danger in Quicksand Swamp
Danger on Panther Peak
[*Original title:* Shadow on the Snow]
A Dog Called Kitty
Eye of the Great Bear
Ferret in the Bedroom, Lizards in the Fridge
The Final Freedom
Journey into Terror
Never Say Quit
Snot Stew
Totally Disgusting!
True Friends
Upchuck and the Rotten Willy
Upchuck and the Rotten Willy: The Great Escape
Upchuck and the Rotten Willy: Running Wild
Watchdog and the Coyotes

Available from MINSTREL BOOKS

**Books by Carol and Bill Wallace**

The Flying Flea, Callie, and Me
That Furball Puppy and Me

Available from MINSTREL BOOKS

**Books by Nikki Wallace**

Stubby and the Puppy Pack

Available from MINSTREL BOOKS

For orders other than by individual consumers, Pocket Books grants a discount on the purchase of **10 or more** copies of single titles for special markets or premium use. For further details, please write to the Vice President of Special Markets, Pocket Books, 1230 Avenue of the Americas, 9th Floor, New York, NY 10020-1586.

For information on how individual consumers can place orders, please write to Mail Order Department, Simon & Schuster, Inc., 100 Front Street, Riverside, NJ 08075.

# BILL WALLACE

# EYE OF THE GREAT BEAR



Aladdin Paperbacks
New York London Toronto Sydney Singapore

This book is a work of fiction. Any references to historical events, real people, or real locales are used fictitiously. Other names, characters, places, and incidents are the product of the author's imagination and any resemblance to actual events or locales or persons, living or dead, is entirely coincidental.

First Aladdin Paperbacks edition February 2002



Originally published in hardcover and paperback in 1999 by Pocket Books

ALADDIN PAPERBACKS
An imprint of Simon & Schuster
Children's Publishing Division
1230 Avenue of the Americas
New York, NY 10020



Also available in a Simon & Schuster Books for Young Readers
hardcover edition.

Printed in the U.S.A.
10 9

ISBN: 0-671-02502-3

*To*

*David and Marcia Hashley*

# EYE OF THE GREAT BEAR

# CHAPTER 1

DADDY WAS BORN ON THE FOURTH OF July. He used to tease us and say he was twelve years old before he finally figured out that everyone wasn't really celebrating *his* birthday.

Daddy loved the Fourth of July.

I hated it.

First off, it was hot. Course, summer is always hot in west Texas. Independence Day, landing right in the middle of summer, well . . . it just seemed to be a lot hotter than most days. All the people crowded around at the carnival didn't help much, either. Then there was Kimmerly. Kimmerly was a pest. Ever since I turned eleven, it seemed like she stuck to me like glue. There was just no shaking her. Mama finally made Kimmerly stay with her so I could have a little time on my own.

Worst of all were the firecrackers. I liked firecrackers. I had fun setting them off. Only when I wasn't thinking about them or watching . . . when some of the other guys—my "friends" from school—found out how I jumped . . . well, I didn't even want to think about it.

The Bill Bently Carnival Show wasn't that bad. They had some jugglers, a camel—which was about the ugliest, weirdest critter we ever saw—a bear in a wagon cage, who managed to spend most of his time sleeping even with all the fireworks going off—and an old Indian medicine man who could guess your age and tell your fortune, both.

We each had a dime. When we finally got to the front of the long line to see the medicine man, my oldest brother, Andrew, and his wife went inside the tepee first. The rest of us hushed up and tried to listen through the thin walls. The medicine man got Andrew's age right on the dot, but missed Deloris's by a year. Then he told them they would be blessed with five children—the first to come next spring. Daniel and his fiancée went in next. He got Daniel's age and Esther's right. He told them that they would be married soon and have five children, too. Patrick was fifteen and was interested in this girl at school named Louise. When he got to go inside, the medicine man told him that he had not met his love yet. She was far away, but he would meet her soon.

The twins, Matthew and Luke, decided to take

their dimes and ride the camel. Andrew tried to tell them that the line was too long, but they wouldn't listen.

As soon as Patrick came out of the tepee, it was my turn to go in. It was dark and smelled of smoke inside. When I walked in and stood, the old man looked up at me. All of a sudden he kind of jerked and struggled to his feet. He motioned me closer to the fire and leaned forward. Soon as our eyes met, he kind of stepped back.

"Some men spend their life searching for who they are—searching for their courage. You will see yourself in the eye of the great bear."

With that he brushed past me, scurried around the edge of the tepee, and disappeared. I just stood there for a time, with my mouth gaping open and feeling downright weird inside. Folks who were still waiting in line were upset. Some of them had been working their way to the front for the better part of an hour. The barker, who was constantly talking and yelling to get people to come and have their fortunes told, smiled and said as how the old man was just taking a little rest. He promised them that he would be right back. Only instead of seeming relaxed about it, the barker looked worried. The guy behind me had already given him his dime. The barker handed it back and scurried off to look for the old medicine man.

I didn't know where the rest of my family went, so I headed straight to the bear wagon. The black, woolly thing was curled up in a corner. I kind of wiggled my way through the crowd of people who had gathered to look at him. I got as close to the end where his head was as I could.

The smell was terrible. It made my nose squeeze shut. And when I did breathe, I didn't take in much air. I looked at him and shrugged. There was no seeing myself in the eye of *this* great bear. That was on account of his eyes were closed.

Right about then, there was this loud *BOOM*. It shook the bars of the cage. Everyone jumped. Some of the old soldiers had set off the Civil War cannon in the Abilene town square. That was the signal for everyone to take blankets or chairs and make their way to the spring down near the pond.

When the cannon went off, the bear lifted his head from the wood plank floor and looked around. For an instant, our eyes met. Only I didn't see myself. All I saw were brown eyes, dull and lifeless. They didn't look at me or focus on anything. He made a *whoompf* sound and put his head back down.

Daddy always said that fortune-tellers were a waste of time and money. Wishing I'd saved my dime to ride the camel with the twins, I shrugged and headed off to find Mama, Daddy, and the rest of my family.

When most of us were settled down by the spring, Iris Levine, the banker, and Dave Abbot, who owned the mercantile, the saloon, and a bunch of other stuff in town, brought big boxes and set them on the pond dam. It was dark by the time they got the fireworks out of the boxes and lined up. Then they lit some cigars and handed them to their kids. The boys started setting off rockets with the cigars. Reckon all of us kids wished we had rockets to set off, but they were the only ones in town who were rich enough to afford such things.

The hot sticky day cooled when the sun went down. Everyone oohed and aahed as we watched the rockets streak into the night sky and explode with sparks all over the place. Soon as the show was done, we walked back to town, climbed aboard our wagon, and headed home.

We had brought the platform spring wagon. It was the only thing big enough to carry the whole family. Daddy drove the four-horse team from the bench seat. Mama sat on the bench, too, with Kimmerly, who was four, smushed in between them. Before we left for town, Daddy had loaded four kitchen chairs in the wagon. Andrew and Deloris sat in the first two. The two behind Andrew and Deloris were for Daniel and Esther. They weren't married yet, but they planned to get hitched this November.

Patrick, who was fifteen, and the twins—who were thirteen, two years older than me—all three sat on the tailboard with their feet dangling. I was between the last two chairs and my brothers on the back, nestled into the pile of blankets and table linen that we used for the church social and for lying on at the fireworks show.

The horses made a steady *clip-clop*—the shod hooves pounding with the slow rhythm of someone drumming their fingers on a table—as we headed home after the big day's celebration. Matthew and Luke told about the camel. Even though they just rode around the little pen, once, they still made it sound fun and exciting. I wished I hadn't wasted my dime on that medicine man and his goofy thing about seeing myself in the eye of the great bear.

After they told their story about the camel, Daddy started in on how they didn't have fireworks back when he was a kid. He told about the cowhands that rode though town, firing their big, old Walker Colts or Dragoons in the air. He told about the church socials, horse races, picnics, and the like. I always enjoyed listening to Daddy's stories.

"In the middle of the Abilene square," he said, "they didn't have the Civil War cannon. The one they had then was left over from the War with Mexico. Half the time when they tried to set it off, the blamed thing wouldn't work. But when it did, the whole town come clean up off their rumps. You talk about loud. Old thing would shake the windows in the storefronts and—"

Matthew leaned over and nudged Luke. "Bet Bailey would still be jumping if that thing went off," he whispered—just loud enough for me to hear him talking about me. Both twins snickered. I bit down on my bottom lip. Before I bit hard enough for it to hurt, I let go and just scooted deeper into the pile of blankets. Maybe if I pretended to be asleep, they'd leave me alone.

The damage was already done. Their words were like a knife twisting into my heart.

Being branded a coward was bad, but having my own brothers feel the same . . . I scrunched my eyes tight as I could. I hated them.

No, I hated me.

Both of them laughed again and glanced back at me.

I waited a minute—maybe two. Then slowly, quietly, I eased around on the blankets. I scooted closer. I tucked my knees up against my chest and wiggled toward them.

Then, when they weren't expecting it, I aimed my feet at the middle of their backs and pushed with all my might.

# CHAPTER 2

DADDY HAD HIS BELT OFF AND WAS standing at the back of the wagon before Matthew and Luke could get to their feet and start after me. He stood between us, with his belt doubled. He flopped it back and forth against his leg so it made a popping sound.

Even in the dark I could see the glare of Matthew's eyes. The white shone like beacons against the black night. He spit dirt and wiped at the blood that dripped from his nose. Thinking about Matthew landing in the dirt on his face made me smile. Luke stood rubbing his bottom with one hand and the back of his head with the other. That made me smile, too.

Daddy didn't smile.

"Don't suppose you two fell asleep and pitched off the wagon by yourselves."

Matthew pointed at me.

"Bailey kicked us," he sniffed, wiping his nose again.

"Shoved us with his feet," Luke whined. "Didn't give us no warning. There weren't no call for it, neither."

Daddy turned to me. I sat, not smiling or frowning either one. Just sat, glaring past him at the twins. Luke stepped to one side, trying to get past Daddy and reach me. Daddy popped the belt harder against his leg.

"You boys didn't do nothing to Bailey?"

"No, sir!" they both echoed at once.

"Didn't hit him or kick him?"

"No, sir!"

"Didn't say nothing to him that caused him to do that?"

When there was no answer, his stare left me and turned to them. "Didn't say nothin'?" Daddy repeated.

"Not to cause him to do what he did," Matthew answered softly. He wiped a finger under his nose and stared at the blood in the moonlight.

"What did you say?"

There was nothing but silence from the twins. Daddy held the buckle and one end of the belt in his right hand. He stuck his left thumb through the loop, jerked real hard so it popped like a gunshot.

"What did you say?"

When they still didn't answer, he glanced at me. Way I had it figured, they were the ones what said it, so they were the ones what needed to 'fess up.

"Teasing him again about the firecracker stuff?"

Both boys looked down. Luke kind of drew a little circle in the dirt with his big toe. Daddy commenced threading his belt back through the loops on his jeans.

"We talked about this last year," he said. "Bailey's your brother. He's *not* a coward. He's just jumpy, that's all. Don't know why, but figure God had his reasons for puttin' springs in Bailey's legs. Whatever the reason, we talked about it and agreed as how brothers take up for one another."

Now both were drawing circles in the dirt.

When Daddy turned back to the wagon seat, Matthew's face kind of lit up. I felt my hands draw to tight fists, ready for their attack. Calm as always, Daddy climbed to the bench seat and took hold of the reins.

"Go right ahead," he said, not so much as glancing back. "Making fun of Bailey because the boys throw firecrackers at him and chase him was wrong. He had every right to take up for himself. Another fight breaks out in the back of this wagon, I'm gonna side with Bailey. It's gonna end up being more than just a little busting."

He popped the horses with the reins. Matthew and Luke stood staring at me as the wagon pulled away.

They were mite near lost in the dark before they started running. They hopped on the tailboard and rode there, mumbling and growling to themselves.

"Tell about the mountains, Daddy," Kimmerly insisted. Balanced on the bench seat, she lay her head in Daddy's lap and put her feet across Mama.

"Tell about the cattle drive, first," Daniel called. "Esther's never heard about that. Have you, Esther."

I knew Deloris had heard the story about the cattle drive, seeing as how she and Andrew lived in the same house with us. I figured Esther had heard it, too. She'd certainly been around long enough. Esther and Daniel had been courting for most of a year now.

"I don't remember hearing the story," Esther answered. "A real cattle drive, Mr. Trumbull? Please tell about it."

I curled up on the blankets again. The twins would get me, that was for sure. But it wouldn't be tonight. They were patient. They'd wait, pick a fight, or blame me for something else next week. It didn't matter. I wasn't afraid of them. I'd take my licking for what I did. I might even get in a few good punches of my own along the way.

"Well, back in the early spring of 1866," Daddy began, "this fella name of Nelson Story rounded up about fifteen hundred head of the nastiest, rankest Texas longhorns you ever set eyes on. His plan was to drive 'em to Montana. There was plenty of land to be had up there. Plenty of free grass, too. I was fourteen way back in sixty-six," Daddy went on. "Been helping my pappy break horses for the army since I was eleven and fancied myself the best bronc buster in all of west Texas. Didn't know a blamed thing about longhorns. But when Story come hunting cowpunchers, I told him I was his man and signed on. We set out on a Friday and . . ."

Daddy's words began to fade with the steady *clip-clop* of the team's hooves. I knew the story about the cattle drive, and my mind began to race ahead of his words.

My daddy was born on the home place, about six miles west of Abilene, Texas. In 1866 he and a bunch of others joined this Story guy for a cattle drive to Montana. Only, instead of coming home after they got the cattle there, he heard word of a gold strike at Confederate Gulch. A lot of the drovers stayed in Montana. Daddy made a pretty fair strike near Pipestone Pass, not far from Billings. During the summer of 1868, he made his way up the North Fork of the Flathead River. He didn't find any gold there, but he did find a mountain valley that he loved. Land was cheap, so he bought the place with part of his gold. But most of his gold he spent to buy cattle and a huge ranch between Great Falls and Helena.

Once he had the ranch up and running, he made his way back to Texas and married Mama. They had been sweethearts in school or something. That was back in 1871. Before he took her to the ranch, they spent a couple of months in a cabin he built up in the mountains. The place didn't have a name—they just called it "their place" out west of the Flathead.

The ranch did right well. Andrew, my oldest brother, was born in 1874 and Daniel was born in 1879. Mama and Daddy had a couple of girls, but they didn't make it. The Northern Pacific Railroad came through in 1883, the same year Patrick was born. Daddy always said that eighty-three through eighty-five were the heydays for Montana ranchers. But the worst winter in Montana history hit in 1886, and when it was all said and done, out of two thousand head of cattle, Mama and Daddy were left with just under three hundred head.

They talked sometimes about that horrible winter. It was the year the twins were born—Matthew and Luke. They were sorry about their life's work being wiped out that winter, but the truth of the matter was—they were happy that they managed to survive and that the twins made it. They sold the ranch and, with what little money they had left, bought the two farms next to the home place back here in Texas. We had seven sections of land. Mama and Daddy had seven of us kids. I was born here in Texas in 1888 and Kimmerly was born in 95. When they quit farming, they always said they'd move back to "their place" near the Flathead. Each of us kids would have a section of land—640 acres—that we could call our own. Daddy said it wasn't much, but if money kept coming in from the three oil wells that pumped on the far west side of our place, we would probably be all right.

My head clunked against the side boards of the wagon. My eyes popped opened, fluttered a couple of times. Must have hit a wheel rut or something, I decided. I nestled my head into the blankets and tried to go back to sleep.

Daddy was still talking about his gold mining days. Since I had already been through his whole story in my head before I fell asleep, my mind wandered on to other things.

Even if it was Daddy's birthday, I hated the Fourth of July.

Last Independence Day, things just sort of happened. This year Emmerson Foster had been laying for me. Soon as I wasn't watching, he pitched a firecracker right on top of my bare foot. Just like last year, I jumped and took off running. Then him and a bunch of other guys from school laughed and threw firecrackers and called me names. Now everybody in town thought I was a coward. It just wasn't fair! Emmerson Foster was a no-account. I knew I could take him.

In my dream, I did. It was a sweet dream, too.

# CHAPTER 3

I WOKE THE NEXT MORNING BEFORE DAY-light. Daddy was always up an hour or two before the sun, but he let the rest of us sleep late—leastwise, until first light. Guess the little naps I took in the wagon left me plenty rested. I got up before anyone else and set out to find Daddy. I needed to talk with him. Just the two of us, with nobody else around.

Figuring he was in the barn, I headed that direction. Near the doorway I could see the glow from the Rochester brass bowl lamps. They had round wicks and gave off considerable more light than the old flat-wick types we used to have when I was little. Like I thought, he was working on the Deering binder-harvester.

It didn't make much sense to me, seeing as how we just finished the first cutting of grass hay. Fact was, we had all of it in the barn, except for a few bundles down by the creek. We'd get that up today, and wouldn't use the Deering again for at least a month. Course, if it didn't rain pretty soon, there wouldn't be another hay cutting. The thing might do nothing but set here until next spring. Still, Daddy always said that you can't let machinery lay around. He was always greasing the pulleys or sharpening the mower blades or tightening the reaper.

"Morning," I greeted.

Daddy jumped and glanced up from filing a sharp edge on one of the twenty or so mower fingers. He smiled when he saw me standing in the doorway.

"You're up mighty early. Late as we got in last night, figured everybody would need to be shook out of bed this morning."

I sat on one of the steel wheels and watched him. "Thought we were working the cotton patch this morning. Shouldn't you be sharpening the hoe, 'stead of messin' with this thing?"

"Sharpened mine yesterday, before we left for town. Got an edge on it that you could shave with. Yours could use a little work."

"I don't shave yet. I'm just eleven."

Daddy looked up and rolled his eyes. He pitched the file to me, got a screwdriver, and went to messing with one of the pulley wheels on the other side of the machine. I knelt down and went to sharpening the mower blade he had been working on. I used one hand to guide and the other hand to push the file across the edge.

"I got up early, 'cause . . . well . . . I was kinda needin' to talk some stuff out . . . sorta."

The pulley wheel he was working on squeaked. Daddy smiled. He dipped his finger in the grease can and dabbed some on the wheel.

"I'm listening," he said when I didn't start in talking.

I gave a little cough. Cleared my throat.

"Well, this thing with the firecrackers is really bothering me. I'm not scared of the things—I swear."

"I know that, Bailey." He wiped some grease on the hay by his foot and moved to the next pulley wheel. "I've seen you set the things off. When you were five, one blew up in your hand. You were little and did some crying and hollering, but within ten minutes you came right back to light another one. If you were scared, you wouldn't do that."

"That's right." I nodded. "I'm not scared. Only, when one of the blamed things goes off by my foot or gets close when I'm not expecting it . . . well . . . I jump, and . . ."

"Once you start jumping, you can't quit," Daddy finished what I was stammering to say.

"Yes, sir. That's what I do."

He dabbed some grease between the cogs of the wheel. Only this time, even when it didn't squeak, he was still frowning.

"If it was just one time—just on the Fourth of July—I could handle it. But it isn't, Daddy. Emmerson and the other guys keep up their teasing and pestering about me jumping and running away all year. They're always calling me a sissy or a coward. Just keep it going and going."

"Emmerson comes by it honest." Daddy dabbed some more grease on the sprocket. "Old man Foster was about the meanest, nastiest critter that ever lit in west Texas. His boy's a pretty nice man, so it must have skipped a generation. The nasty lit on Emmerson, his grandson. But what I can't figure is why you let it bother you. You know what kind of boy he is. Nobody's got much respect for him, so why does it bother you what he thinks?"

"He gets the other guys doing it, too."

"So? Long as you know you aren't a coward, what does it count what others think? Long as a man knows what's true, nobody else should matter."

"But it does matter." I clamped my lips together and sucked in a deep breath.

Daddy looked up and studied me for a long time. Finally he sighed. I sniffed again. He wiped the grease off his hand, came over, and took the file from me. I scooted aside, folded my legs under me, and plopped down on the hay-covered floor. Without looking at me, he started filing.

"When I was a kid, I was scared of horses."

I felt my mouth fall open. "I thought you used to break horses with your dad."

"I did." He nodded. "When I was eleven. Before then, I steered clear of the stupid beasts. Pappy tried to talk me over it. Had a gentle mare named Sally that he used to let me ride. I was still scared.

"One day he had a friend of his come over. A full-blood Comanche name of White Corn. Never did find out how come Pappy and old White Corn were friends. Back in those days the Comanche and the Texans was still fighting one another." He kind of stared off at the top of the barn, thinking—remembering. Then he shrugged and smiled back at me. "Anyhow, the two of 'em threw a loop over this wild mare, eared her down, and put a saddle on her. Then they threw me on her back and let her go."

"What happened."

"Got throwed off. Landed right on my bottom, and while they was catching her again, I took off for the trees to hide out."

I shook my head. It was hard to believe that my daddy was ever scared of anything, much less that he'd try to run away from something.

"So what happened?"

"Took ole White Corn less than ten minutes to track me down. Stuck me under his arm like he was carrying a bedroll, and took me back to my pappy. Pitched me back on the old horse again."

I felt my eyebrows go up. "You rode her, this time. Right?"

"Nope. Threw me on my face the second time. Third time they put me on her, I went through the fence. After that I don't remember where or how I landed. But somewhere along the line—someplace between all the dirt and dust and bleeding and hurting . . . well, I ended up being so mad at that stupid horse for throwing me, I forgot how scared I was. When I had the pitch rode out of her, I went hunting another horse to break. Way I got it figured, we might try the same kind of thing with you."

I frowned and cocked my head to the side.

"Huh?"

Daddy almost laughed when he looked at me. He shook his head and smiled.

"Not throwing you on a horse. You got any fire-crackers left over from yesterday?"

"Yes, sir."

"I know Patrick and the twins do. What we're gonna do—" He broke off what he was saying and made a grunting sound when he got to his feet. With a smile, he ran his thumb down the edge of the mower tooth. "Now understand, I don't want to do this. Like I told you last year and like I told the twins—I don't know why the good Lord put springs in your legs, but I'm sure he had a reason. I truly do hate to try and change what was intended. But seein' as how it's bothering you so much . . . well . . . the

Fourth of July is gonna last a mite longer this year than normal.

"We're gonna get the whole family in on it. Might even send Andrew to town for more firecrackers. Don't know how long it's gonna take, but whether you're working or sittin' in the shade or taking care of business in the outhouse, somebody's gonna have a firecracker ready to go off when you're not expecting it. Sooner or later you'll get so mad at yourself or us, or just get so tired of jumping that it'll quit."

I stood up straight and took a deep breath. I felt my chest swell. My spirits kind of swelled, too. It sounded like a great plan. I dreaded it, but it would work. I just knew it.

Probably would have, too, if it weren't for that darned rattlesnake.

•

# CHAPTER 4

CHOPPING COTTON IS HARD WORK. IT GETS your back because you have to spend so much time bent over. First off, you got to lean down to find the weeds or goatheads or grass under the cotton leaves. Then you have to reach low on the hoe handle so you can whack the weeds without cutting down the young cotton plant.

Daddy wasn't happy when you clipped the cotton instead of the weeds.

It was almost noon when he called a halt to it.

"No more firecrackers in the cotton patch," he announced. "Bailey's not jumping as high or far as he did this morning. But every time one goes off, he cuts down a couple of plants. We're not gonna have a cotton crop if this keeps up."

I straightened and rubbed my back. Daddy and

each of us boys took two rows at a time. When we got to the end of the row, we skipped over the rows someone else had done or was working on, and went to the next two.

I could sure tell the rows I'd been chopping. They were ragged as could be, with big holes or gaps where there was no cotton plant left. I could almost tell from the dead plants how many firecrackers my daddy and brothers threw at me.

We finished the rows we were on, then headed to the house early. That was on account of Kimmerly.

Chopping cotton has to be done in the middle of summer. That's when cotton grows. Naturally, that's when weeds grow, too. Long about midmorning Kimmerly was supposed to fetch us some drinking water from the spring. When she didn't show, we weren't surprised. Kimmerly was only four. That and the fact that Mama and Daddy spoiled her rotten . . . well, she just didn't always do what she was supposed to.

What bothered us was that Kimmerly never seemed to get in trouble for it. I can remember when I was little, I had chores to do—just like the rest of the family. Forget, and it was Daddy's belt or you ended up doing extra chores. When Kimmerly didn't do something . . . well . . .

Reckon her being the only girl in a family of six boys had something to do with it, too. The first child Mama and Daddy had was a girl. She was born in 1872, one year to the day after they were married.

They named her Mary. She was only two days old when she died. Danielle was born in 1876. The fever took her, just a few days shy of her first birthday. Then there was another girl in 1880 that Mama said was "stillborn."

Even Andrew and Daniel spoiled Kimmerly. Guess they were around when Mama and Daddy lost Danielle and the other little girl. Guess they knew how much Kimmerly meant to Mama and Daddy.

I knew it, too, only it still bothered me when she got away with stuff.

Anyhow, we were all about to die of thirst, so we headed off early for the spring and for dinner. Our spring was a work of art if there ever was one. Nothing more than a steady stream of water that oozed from the brown Texas sand, Daddy and the boys had rocked it the year I was born. Well, Daddy, Andrew, and Daniel rocked it. The twins weren't quite two years old and Andrew told me once that Patrick was only four. He and Daddy laughed about how Patrick threw more rocks at the creek than he helped pile in the spring.

Daddy got the idea for our spring from "their place" in Montana. The basin in that high, mountain valley where he and Mama spent their honeymoon had a spring just like ours—only it was natural.

From the stories they told, I reckon they both loved the place. Seemed like every time they got the chance, they sneaked off and went there to spend some time. Well, every chance they got up until 1886. It was that winter when the blizzards came and they lost most everything.

After they sold the ranch and paid to ship the few cows that made it through the winter back here to Texas, there was no money left for house lumber. Daddy and my older brothers cut their own. They split the logs with a froe. That's sort of a T-shaped chisel, with the cutting edge along the top bar of the *T*. They augered holes and used wood pegs—built our whole house without one single nail. When they were done with the house, and before they started on the barn, they fixed the spring.

And like I said, it was a work of art.

A row of rocks, about as wide as both my hands together, stretched from where the water oozed out of the ground and led into a little pool. The pool was about three feet around and three feet deep. But the water was so clean and clear, the pebbles on the bottom seemed like they were only an inch or so under the surface. When that pool filled, the water trickled over a couple of big rocks and down a steep slope into another pool. That pool was over twice as big around. In the middle it was probably as deep as I was tall, but on the sides, there was a ledge or rim of rocks that I could sit on. Down below that was still a third pool. It was about the same size as the top pool. Surrounding the whole thing was a rock wall about five foot high and a wood gate. That was to keep out the cattle and any other big critters.

The big pool, or the middle one, was our bathing water. Mama was a real stickler when it came to cleanliness. One of her favorite quotes was: "Cleanliness is next to Godliness." Each day after work we had to pitch into the big pool, scrub down with lye soap, and wash clean before we came to the house for supper. The bottom pool was where she and Deloris washed the clothes. The top pool was our drinking water.

When we got there, the gourd dipper was beside the spring, but there was no water bucket and *no* Kimmerly.

Even though we were thirsty as could be, everybody spread out, searching for her before we so much as got a drink. Don't know what it is about little ones, but when they're quiet for a long while, or when you expect to see them someplace and they aren't there . . . well . . . it kind of yanks a knot in your stomach and sets your head whipping all around trying to spot them.

Not being able to see Kimmerly right off left a right cold feeling on my insides and kind of bristled the hair at the back of my neck.

Daddy was the one who found her.

# CHAPTER 5

KIMMERLY WAS ABOUT A HUNDRED YARDS down the creek from the spring. Even that far away, we could see the mud. Her long dress, her sunbonnet, her—everything was covered.

Daddy went to fetch her while the rest of us passed the gourd, then moved down to wash off in the big pool.

"She's gonna get it this time," Patrick said, splashing water on his face and neck.

Luke nodded. "Sure wouldn't want to be in her shoes when Daddy gets hold of her."

Kimmerly was all excited when Daddy brought her back to the spring. He carried Kimmerly in one hand and our good water bucket in the other. We each had to look into the bucket to see what she had.

It was unbelievable!

Our good water bucket—all clean and fresh as the drinking pool, our only good water bucket with new wood and fresh tar—it was half full of mud and crawdads. The nasty little things climbed and crawled all over one another. They snapped with their pincers and in general totally mucked up a perfectly good bucket.

Kimmerly thought they were cute.

Daddy thought Kimmerly was cute.

Luke looked at Matthew and me. All three of us rolled our eyes. We knew good and well if we'd done that, Daddy would have skinned our hides.

Daddy even let Kimmerly bring the water bucket, full of crawdads, to the house so she could show Mama and Deloris.

After dinner we took turns in the outhouse before going back to work. I waited until last. Even after a good dinner and relaxing in the cool breeze that swept through the dog-trot, I still felt all tight and jittery inside. The dog-trot was the open area between the kitchen and the bedroom part of our Texas-style home. It was covered with the roof that connected the cooking area and the sleeping area. During the heat of the day, it was about the only cool place on the whole spread.

Once sure that everybody else had taken care of their business, I looked both ways and headed out to take care of mine. I figured if I let them get back to the cotton patch, I wouldn't have to jump at fire-crackers every step of the way.

When I finished, I peeked through the new moon cut in the wood door. There was nobody around. I stretched my neck outside and looked both directions. There was nobody lurking there with fire-crackers. I was feeling real safe and relaxed when I started through the doorway. That's when the fire-cracker came flying over the top of the outhouse. When it went off, I jumped. When I jumped, I clunked my head on the piece of wood above the outhouse door.

Patrick, Matthew, and Luke laughed so hard, I thought they were going to fall over and roll on the ground. I rubbed my head and growled at them a little. Only, I really couldn't get too mad. Guess it *was* kind of funny. My head hurt, my legs were tired, and my insides felt like a long-tailed cat in a room full of rocking chairs. Still, the good side of it was that Matthew and Luke were so busy pestering me that they plum forgot about getting even for me shoving them out of the wagon.

We finished the cotton patch, and long about dark Daddy got to feeling sorry for me, I guess. Between chopping cotton and jumping, I was plum worn down to a frazzle. He told me to come with him and help fetch the last of the grass hay to the barn. He sent my brothers on to take a bath and go to the house.

We hitched Jumper and Whitey to the platform spring wagon. Daddy said that with no more hay than there was, we only needed two horses. Daddy drove the team and I sat beside him on the bench seat, flipping Whitey in the rump with pebbles. Whitey was kind of a slacker. You didn't keep him moving and he'd lag back and let Jumper pull the whole load by himself.

I flipped another pebble and looked over to Daddy.

"Don't think it's working." I sighed.

Daddy shrugged.

"You ain't jumping as high as you was this morning."

I gave a little snort. "That's only on account of being so tired. I'm still jumpy inside. Legs just so weak they can't get me off the ground."

Daddy smiled when he reached over with a big, callused hand to ruffle my hair.

"It might take time, Bailey, but it'll work. Fact is, think I'll send Andrew to town so he can fetch us more firecrackers. Let's give it a few more days, what do you think?"

I felt my mouth twist up on one side.

"Whatever."

The Deering harvester-binder left the grass in clumps with string tied around them. Daddy stopped the team beside the first pile. He got his pitchfork and walked out a ways. I started on the grass nearest the wagon. Figuring I could pick up more in my arms, I leaned the pitchfork against the wagon, reached down, and scooped up an armload.

I hadn't even straightened when I heard the buzz.

West Texas has rattlesnakes. There are plenty of them—that's just a fact. Only at eleven years old, I'd never seen one.

Well, I'd seen chopped ones. Andrew found one down by the spring and smashed it with a rock. Mama had chopped two, just this year. One was out by the chicken house, the other by the woodpile. But the only ones I had ever seen were already dead. Never saw a live one, much less heard one rattle.

Something inside me knew the sound.

My eyes shot to the side, under the pile of hay I'd just lifted. The thing was big. Real big. He whipped himself into a pile of coils wrapping and gathering in a circle. In less time than it took me to blink, his ugly head reared from the coils. I could see his forked tongue lash out. I was close enough to see the ridge that made it look like he had horns over his eyes.

Less than two feet away, I even saw the long, sharp fangs when he struck.

Mama was suspicious when we showed up at the supper table without stopping by the spring first. The fact that Daddy was as white as a sheet and his eyes were sort of bugged out might have tipped her off, too.

She knew something was going on, only she didn't say anything. Reckon the rest of the family felt something was amiss, as well. But like Mama, they kept it to themselves. Everyone just watched Daddy and me, and waited.

Daddy said grace over the food, but when he was done, he didn't pass the plates. He just sat there. Like everybody else, I watched him. Daddy took a deep breath. He opened his mouth like he was going to say something, then he gave a little shudder—like a cold chill was racing up his back. He waited awhile and drew another deep breath.

"Only seen the like once in my life," he began, his voice real soft. "Old-time gunslinger by the name of Sid Burke was on the cattle drive with Nelson Story and the rest of us. Evenings, after we settled the cattle down, he'd get out of earshot from the herd. He'd find a real snakey-looking bluff and start flipping rocks over with his boot. If there was a rattler under one, he'd draw and shoot before it struck. Said it helped keep his gun hand and his shootin' eye honed to a sharp edge."

He gave another little shudder. "But even Sid Burke didn't try to beat a strike. It can't be done. A rattlesnake can strike quicker than a man can blink. Even Sid drew down on them before they struck."

He made a gulping sound and pointed to me. "Bailey picked up an armload of hay, down by the creek. Big old diamondback was under it."

I heard Mama moan. Deloris covered her eyes with her hand.

"Bailey was about a foot and a half away when I heard it rattle. I didn't even have time to yell when I saw him coil. I saw the rattlesnake raise his head. Saw Bailey's leg. Saw him strike."

# CHAPTER 6

"GOT NO IDEA," I SAID. IT WAS THE ONLY truthful answer I could give. "I really don't know. The only thing I can figure was that my feet jumped when they heard him rattle and I was already leaving the ground when Daddy seen him strike. But . . . honest, I don't remember. I heard him rattle. I saw him. Next thing I knew, I was in the back of the wagon and Daddy was doin' him in with the pitchfork. Musta really been in the air and it all happened so fast, Daddy just thought I . . ."

Daddy shook his head so hard, his ears almost flopped.

"No, Bailey. I seen it. Seen it with my own eyes. You were flatfooted and that rattler's fangs were out. His head was moving. Next second, you were gone and his strike went right under your bare foot. You it the ground and before he coiled and struck again, ou jumped clean up in the air and lit in the wagon. saw it. I saw it with my own two eyes!"

All I could do was shrug. Fact of the matter, I hrugged so hard that I felt my ears go clean down etween my shoulders.

"Like I said, I don't remember. But if that's what ou saw . . ."

After we finished supper, Daddy took a lantern nd he and I went to wash up before bed. He was ight cautious about where we stepped. He even nade a couple of circles around the bathing pool efore we got in and bathed.

The whole family had settled down for bed when ve heard the triangle clanging. The triangle was kind f our dinner bell. It was nothing more than a small ron triangle that dangled from the roof of our porch n the end of a rawhide string. An iron rod hung ext to it. Sometimes, when we were out in the field nd Mama had dinner ready before we came to the ouse, she'd ring it to tell us to get home. Mostly it ust hung there, and the only time it clanged was hen there was a strong wind.

When the house was first built, it was what was alled a Texas style. One part for the cooking and ating, an open area (or dog-trot) covered by the oof, then the sleeping area. Now, it was what folks alled a shotgun house. That was a house all strung together like beads on a string. Mama and Daddy built another sleeping room just for us boys. It was next to theirs and there was a dog-trot in between. When Andrew got married, they built another dog-trot and sleeping house on the far side of the kitchen. Now that Daniel was fixing to get hitched, we had already started on another sleeping house on the other side of Andrew and Deloris's room. Come September, there would be five houses, all hitched together and under one roof.

When we heard the *clang, clang, clang* of the triangle, we all jumped up and come a-runnin'. Daddy stood in the dog-trot by the kitchen in his nightshirt. Deloris was pulling on her robe when she came from the other side of the kitchen, and Kimmerly yawned and scratched her bottom.

"What is it, Daddy?" We all seemed to ask at once. "What happened? What's going on."

Daddy let go of the iron rod. He stood in the dog-trot and looked at his family, standing in the yard.

"Been doing considerable thinking on this matter." He announced. "Each of you know that I believe a man's only as good as his word. The one thing stronger than a man's word is a sign from God."

Now our daddy wasn't the religious sort. I mean he wasn't a heathen or nothing like that, but Mama did most of our religious training. She was the one what made sure we got to church, come Sunday morning. She was the one who read to us from the

Bible. Daddy made it to church sometimes. Sometimes he didn't. Our daddy wasn't much for seeing signs from God, neither.

Mama and Daddy had a wisteria bush outside their bedroom window. Daddy's mom had given it to them when they first moved back to Texas from Montana. For eleven years the thing had grown. It was green and bushy and had climbed clean to the top of the house. But in all that time, there had never been so much as one, single, hangy-down, purple blossom on the thing. Never. Not until two days after Grandma died.

Daddy saw it when we came back from the funeral. He brought us all to the side of the house to show us. He was smiling, but there were tears leaking from his eyes when he pointed it out. He said that his mom always apologized 'cause there weren't any flowers on the wisteria bush she gave them. He said that she was in heaven now, and she was just letting us know that she was all right.

It was the only time I ever saw my daddy cry.

The second he mentioned something about a sign from God, all of us shushed up. We kind of held our breath and leaned forward, listening for what he was to say next.

Instead of saying anything, he stepped down from the dog-trot. He walked over and put an arm around my shoulder.

"It bothers Bailey that the kids from school throw

firecrackers at him and laugh and chase him when he jumps and runs. I told him I'd help him get over it. I was even planning to send Andrew to town to fetch more firecrackers tomorrow." He looked down at me and hugged me tighter. "Bailey, I gave you my word. Now, I'm taking it back. That rattlesnake was a sign. Told you before that I didn't know why the good Lord put springs in your legs, but I hated to try and change what was intended. Maybe this is what was meant to be.

"When school starts, if Emmerson Foster teases you, you'll just have to take it like a man. Next Independence Day, if the guys chase you with firecrackers, you'll just have to take that, too. No matter what I said, I'm not gonna try and change what God intended."

Well, so much for our plan.

In a way I was a little disappointed. In another way . . . well, there was no arguing with Daddy's thinking. Maybe I was meant to be the way I was.

Daddy cut the rattles off the snake's tail and gave them to me for a keepsake. I put them in my pocket but after a couple of days, they got to stinking, so I put them in the cigar box under my bed.

Things went pretty much back to normal. It was chores every day, church on Sundays, then back to chopping cotton and feeding the chickens, cleaning the barn, and all our other chores, come Monday.

Two days after the snake thing, a big thunderstorm rolled through. There wasn't much wind, but it rained something fierce. Daddy went out and worked on his machinery and the rest of us got to just lay around for two whole days. Looked like, come August, we'd get at least one more hay cutting.

About a week after the storm, Luke caught me one evening down by the spring. He looked around, making sure no one else was listening. He kind of eased up to me and spoke real quiet.

"Were you scared, Bailey?"

"Huh?" I frowned.

"When the snake almost bit you. Were you scared?"

"Reckon so." I nodded. "But it was only after we were driving the team back home and I had a chance to think about it. At the time . . ." I shook my head and shrugged. "It all happened so quick I didn't have time to be scared. Not until it was done over with."

I *was* scared, too. Fact, the more I thought about it, the more I realized just how scary almost getting struck by a rattlesnake really was.

But if I thought I was scared about that, it was nothing compared to the scare we took the second week in August.

# CHAPTER 7

THE SECOND TUESDAY IN AUGUST WE were back in the hay field. To be real honest, I was right happy about it. Hauling hay was hard work and real hot, but I didn't mind. That was on account of Kimmerly.

For two weeks after the rattlesnake almost got me, there was no shaking Kimmerly. She hung around me almost all the time—except in the hay field. I couldn't even feed the chickens without stepping on her. She had to sit next to me at dinner, and every night at bedtime she came in our room and gave me a big hug and kiss and told me she was glad the snake didn't eat me. I told her that snakes didn't eat people. She didn't listen. She just hugged and kissed me. The sweet little hugs weren't that bad. But she always managed to get the side of my cheek wet when she kissed. I would just sit and smile at her until she went back to bed. Then I'd wipe my cheek off.

The whole day was unusual hot, even for August. The thing that made it seem worse was that the wind wasn't blowing. The wind always blows in west Texas. Only, there was no wind—not that day.

Last week Daddy and Andrew took turns driving the horses around the hay field. The Deering binder-harvester that they dragged behind the team cut the tall, grass hay and left it in neat rows—all bound up with string. After the rattlesnake thing, Daddy told us we had to use pitchforks—no picking up bundles with our hands. We let the hay cure or dry Friday, Saturday, and on Sunday, too, while we were in church. Come Monday, Andrew and Daniel drove the team and wagon to the barn and threw or forked the hay bundles up to the loft. There, Daddy and Patrick used their pitchforks to move the bundles back and keep a clear path for more hay. Matthew, Luke, and I stayed in the field, piling up the bound hay. That way it was easier to pitch into the wagon.

By Tuesday we had it about half done. Mama and Deloris were frying chicken and taters. Esther got to come over for the day, and she was setting the table and fixing tea. Kimmerly was supposed to be with them, only Kimmerly never stayed much where she was supposed to.

She was the one who found Daddy. How—I don't

know. And why she come running to me instead of to Mama or Andrew . . . well, I don't know that neither.

One minute I was minding my own business, piling hay and wiping sweat from my forehead with my shirtsleeve. The next Kimmerly was slapping me on the back so hard it stung and motioning for me to follow her. She didn't even say nothing, just kept whacking me and waving her arm.

Kimmerly was about the biggest pest there was. Most times I would have backhanded her for hitting me. Only this time—something about the look on her face or the tears in her eyes—this time I just dropped my pitchfork and chased after her.

Daddy was at the edge of the cotton field. The hoe lay beside him on the ground. He was as white as death.

I dropped to my knees beside him and leaned my ear near his lips. I couldn't hear any breath coming in and out. I pressed my ear against his chest. I couldn't hear the pounding of his heart. I rocked back on my heels. Looked at him. His color was a ghostly white, almost gray.

I knew my Daddy was dead.

I don't even remember yelling for help. But I must have. And that yell must have come clean from the heels of my bare feet—not from my throat or chest nor even way down deep in my belly, but clean from my heels. Because Matthew and Luke heard it, way out in the hay field, and come a-runnin'. Andrew, Daniel, and Patrick were all three in the hayloft. They come a-runnin', too. I sent Kimmerly to fetch Mama from the house. Later she told me that Mama and the girls were already past the gate by the time she got across the creek.

Luke was the first to reach us, and Matthew was only a couple of strides behind. But like me, all they could think to do for Daddy was stand and yell for help. Andrew got there next. He shoved the twins aside and dropped to his knees beside Daddy. He yelled at him to wake up, then he shook his shoulders and yelled again.

Daddy didn't move.

Andrew lifted his head and patted him on the cheek. "Wake up, Daddy." He patted his cheek a little harder. "Come on. Wake up!" Andrew patted his cheek so hard it was more like a slap.

When Daddy moaned, my heart might near leaped clean out of my throat. I was still scared and worried, but hearing a sound from him . . . knowing he was alive . . . well . . .

The hope and happy jumped in for only a second. Then the scared chased it away again.

Andrew rolled him from one side to the other, to see if he was hurt anyplace.

Matthew looked at me, then back at Daddy. "Reckon he's snake bit?"

Andrew pulled his pant legs up and looked there. He grabbed Daddy's shirt up near the collar and yanked. He didn't take his shirt off, he ripped it off. We all looked him over as Andrew pushed and tugged him from side to side. There were no holes. No fang marks. Andrew lifted his head and started patting his cheek again.

"What happened?" Mama was puffing and out of breath.

"Don't know." Andrew shook his head. "Bailey and Kim found him. Can't see that he's hurt no place. Not snake bit. He won't wake up!"

Mama dropped to her knees on the other side of Daddy. "John, what's wrong?" she pleaded. "What is it, John? We can't help you 'less you talk to us. Wake up! Talk to me!"

Daddy kind of moaned again.

Suddenly a strange look swept across Mama's face. She put her hand on Daddy's forehead. Frowned. The frown drew deeper lines in her face when she looked around, found his shirt on the ground, and felt of it.

"He's burning up, but he's dry as a bone." Her upper lip kind of stretched down and she nibbled on it with her lower teeth. "Shirt is even dry."

She looked at Andrew, then quickly scanned the rest of us. We were all dripping sweat. Hot as it was and hard as we'd been working, not only our shirts but our pants—at least down to the knees—were as wet as could be.

She frowned back at Daddy. "T'ain't right. Ought to be sweatin'. Just ain't right . . ."

Suddenly she blinked. Her head kind of whipped around toward the creek.

"The spring!" she shouted. "Get him to the spring!"

Mama tried to lift his shoulders, but Andrew nudged her aside. The instant he got Daddy under both arms, Daniel and Patrick reached down and took hold to lift his back and hips. I started for his feet, but Matthew and Luke pushed me back and picked him up. Mama led the way to our spring. About halfway down the hill, she stopped and turned.

"Bailey. Fetch Doc Harrison!"

My feet took over, just like always, and I was gone before the end of "Harrison" left her lips.

It never occurred to me that taking one of the horses would be faster. Never entered my mind that it was a six-mile run to Doc Harrison's office above the Abilene Mercantile. Didn't even think about it being the hottest day of August. I just ran. My bare feet pounded the hard, Texas dirt. That and my breathing were the only sounds I could hear. I ran harder. Soon the sound of my heart pounding echoed inside my head. I sucked deeper breaths. Pushed myself. Ran harder.

Inside my head, words pounded louder than my heart or my feet hitting the ground. The words even drowned out the raspy sound of my ragged breathing.

"Fetch Doc Harrison! Fetch Doc Harrison. Fetch Doc . . ."

# CHAPTER 8

I WAS SOMEWHERE SHY OF BEING HALF-way to town when Delbert Hawkins stopped me. Delbert and his wife, Melinda, were our nearest neighbors. They were coming home from the Mercantile with a wagon load of supplies when they spotted me.

Guess I would have run right past them if Mr. Hawkins hadn't kept yelling and finally jumped down from the wagon seat.

"What's wrong, Bailey?" He grabbed me by the shoulders and hung on.

"Daddy . . . he's bad sick. . . ." I wheezed, struggling for air. "Got to get . . . Doc Harrison. Quick and . . ."

He latched on to my arm and dragged me back to the front of the wagon. "Take ole Thistle. He'll run faster without the wagon. Get that buckle strap. I'll unfasten this one."

Doc Harrison was with Westley Davis when I burst into his second-floor office. Westley had his shirt off and was sitting on the wood examining table.

"Daddy's bad sick!" I blurted, still so out of breath I could barely speak. "Come quick . . . got to help him!"

Doc Harrison grabbed his black bag and pitched it to me. Then we both spun and headed for his buggy.

I put the black bag under the seat and hopped in. I was so scared, I didn't know what to do. I felt myself tremble. It was the hottest day of the year, and I'd just run three miles, then ridden three miles at a dead-out gallop. Still, I was so scared and worried about Daddy, I couldn't keep from shivering.

Doc Harrison unwrapped the reins from the hitching post. His paint gelding was always hitched and ready. He kept him and the buggy tied to the rail near the bottom step, just in case of such emergencies. I scooted over a bit and patted the seat beside me. Doc Harrison put his foot on the buggy, but instead of hopping in, he stood there and watched me a second.

"That Delbert Hawkins's horse?" Mr. Davis called from the top step. He was still wrestling with his shirt.

"Yes, sir." I called back to him. I felt my shoulders

kind of pinch together with another shiver. "They caught me on the road and made me take him."

Mr. Davis yanked and twisted until he had his right arm into his shirtsleeve. "He's pretty lathered up. I'll wipe him down and water him. Tell Delbert I'll fetch him and their wagon, directly."

I gave a quick nod. Another little tremble took hold of my shoulders when I patted the seat beside me once more.

"Come on, Doc. Hurry."

Doc Harrison cocked his head to the side and frowned. I frowned back at him. Shuddered. His eyes squinted down.

"Get off the buggy."

"Huh?"

"Get off."

"But . . . Daddy. He's bad sick. We got to hurry." Confused, I looked around. "Mr. Davis said he'd bring the horse. I'll ride with you so I can show you where they are."

Doc Harrison shook his head. He pointed to the front of the Mercantile. "Hop down and go get in the horse trough, first. Don't like the looks of you. Got yourself way too hot."

"But there's no time—" I broke off, trembling and shaking. "We got to go. Come on!"

Doc Harrison was about the sweetest, gentlest old man anyone could ever meet—especially when it came to dealing with us kids. He never had a gruff word. He was always calm and easy. With his manner, shoot, we weren't even afraid of going to get a shot. Guess that's why it surprised me so when he walked around the buggy, reached up, and latched onto my wrist. He *yanked* me clean off the seat.

I would have landed on my face in the dirt if he hadn't hung on to me. He gave another yank and turned me so I was facing him.

"You're starting the heat sickness. Go get in the horse trough, now, or we ain't going no place."

"But Daddy . . . he . . ."

"He's bad sick. I know. But I need to worry about him when we get to your place. I don't need two sick Trumbulls to worry about. Go plop your butt in the trough. I'll fetch the horse and buggy. Soon as you cool down, we'll be on our way."

I felt the fool.

Daddy was sick and probably dying. And me—I was sitting in a horse trough, on Main Street. Folks what knew me strolled past, kind of smiled or chuckled, and said, "Hi, Bailey." Other folks just stared.

Then I saw Emmerson Foster and the gang of trouble he usually ran with. They were at the far end of the street. I scrunched lower in the warm, slimy water, hoping they wouldn't spot me. When Emmerson smiled and raised up on his tiptoes, I knew it was no use. They started in my direction.

Doc Harrison pulled up in his buggy. When I started to get out of the water, he hopped down and shoved my head under. I came up, coughing and sputtering. The water was warm and the sides of the wood trough were covered with green slime.

Emmerson and the other boys veered off when they saw Doc Harrison. I latched on to the sides of the trough and started to pull myself up. Doc held me down.

"Give it a couple more minutes." he smiled. "Then we'll be on our way."

He finally let me up. Water dripping and green slime sloshing from the leg of my Levi's, I hopped on the buggy seat. My bottom hadn't even touched the pad when he slapped leather to the paint gelding and we flew off in a cloud of dust.

They had Daddy in the dog-trot when we got there. He was sitting in a chair, and Mama and Deloris stood on either side, fanning him with their sunbonnets. Doc Harrison yanked the reins, and the paint gelding slid to a stop. He chased us kids off as well as Mr. and Mrs. Hawkins, who had left their supplies on the wagon and walked to the house to see if they could help. Once everybody but Mama and Daddy were out of the way, he commenced talking with them. After a time it seemed more like he was arguing with Daddy, instead of talking.

We kind of clumped together, down toward the creek, so we could see. Kimmerly sneaked off from us and went to the house. Mama ran her away. When she tried it again, Mrs. Hawkins caught her and held on to her until Doc Harrison waved us back to the house.

"Heat sickness," he announced. "I've seen three cases of it this last week. Old man Fergus, over by Baird, died of heat sickness two days ago. Figure your dad came mite close. If Ruth hadn't gotten him in the spring as quick as she did and brought his temperature down . . . well, he most likely wouldn't be listening to this conversation, right now."

"He gonna be okay?" Andrew asked.

"He had a close call, but I think he's gonna be okay *if* . . ."

We all sort of leaned closer, listening for what was to come after the "if."

"Old man Fergus was in his late fifties," Daddy butted in. "I'm still young, compared to him and—"

"John," Doc Harrison growled, cutting him off. "Age don't make a bit of difference." He jabbed a finger toward me. "Shoot, Bailey had the start of heat sickness when he got to my office. He's only eleven. I had to stick him in the horse trough so he'd cool off before we headed out here. No matter what the age, there's still only one way to treat it and keep it from killin' ya.

"Now, if you don't want to listen to me, *fine!* Go on back to the hay field or up in the loft and see how long you last. Ruth and the kids will be okay. Got some money coming in from those oil wells.

Boys can take care of the farm and take care of their mother. She'll have everything she needs—except you. Now shush up and let me speak my piece. Got other folks what need tending to."

Daddy folded his arms and huffed back into his chair. Doc Harrison looked at him and shook his head. Finally he turned to us.

"First off, he's not to do any work for the next couple of weeks. And I *do* mean *nothing.* After that, if he wants to go out early of a morning or late in the afternoon and do a little, that's okay. But you got to watch him and make sure he doesn't break a sweat. Once the heat sickness gets hold of a fella, it can come back right quick."

He leaned forward, focusing his eyes on me.

"Bailey, you're not to do anything for two days. You understand me?"

"Yes, sir."

"We caught Bailey early. The rest of you—you get to feeling hot or sick to your stomach or dizzy—quit what you're doing and head for the creek. Cool off and drink plenty of water. You get the chills, head for the creek, then quit for the day. You feel sick to your stomach, get the chills, and keep right on working in this heat, next thing you know you stop sweating. Do that and you're in trouble. You'll be in the same fix as your dad. Only most people what get the heat sickness that bad don't live to tell about it." He strolled to his buggy and climbed up on the padded seat. "You boys got to make him mind, ya hear?"

Us kids would have had more luck making snow fall from the sky in August than we did making Daddy mind.

For the first week he did pretty much like Doc Harrison said. The second week he went right back to working like he always had. He told us he was over it and to leave him alone. When we insisted, he'd just growl at us and do what he darned well pleased.

Mama had better luck, but not much. Until . . .

# CHAPTER 9

LONG AS I COULD REMEMBER, SATURDAY was grocery day. We were only six miles from Abilene, so Mama always hitched up the buckboard and took off for town early each Saturday morning. Now that Andrew was married, Deloris went with her to stock in supplies for the week.

Only this week, instead of taking the buckboard, they went out to the barn and hitched up the platform spring wagon. Nobody thought much about it until they came home that afternoon with the week's groceries.

Thing was, along with the flour and molasses and coffee and sack of sugar, they also had four big steamer trunks piled on the flat bed.

We were at the top side of the cotton patch when they came down the road from town. Cotton was easier to chop in late August. The plants were bigger and it wasn't so easy to accidentally chop one. The leaves were beginning to spread out and that shaded the grass and weeds—kept junk from growing up in the rows. From the top side of the patch, we could see the road. We all stopped and looked. I had to squint against the afternoon sun, and it took me a while to make out just what Mama and Deloris had on the back of the wagon. I still didn't think much about it.

Guess Daddy did. He spent a long time leaning on his hoe handle and studying things. Daddy never leaned on his hoe. Said it was made for choppin' and not for resting. Even so, Daddy spent a long, *long* time hanging on that handle and frowning at the wagon.

We finished the cotton and went to the spring to wash for supper. Andrew, being the oldest, always put the buckboard in the barn and turned the horses into the pasture when Mama came home after Saturday shopping. The platform spring wagon was unloaded when we got to the house, but Andrew didn't even look at the horses, much less put them up. Daddy didn't either.

"Reckon we ought to put the horses in the pen?" I asked Daniel.

He didn't even glance at me, just brushed on past and followed Andrew and Daddy into the house.

"The horses, Patrick? Reckon we ought to . . ."

He was hot on Daniel's heels.

"Horses?" That's all I got out of my mouth when Luke and Matthew disappeared through the door.

Not wanting to be left out, I shrugged and chased after them.

Dinner wasn't quite ready, so each of us sat at our place around the table. Nobody said much. Mama and Deloris set plates around, then put the food down and sat. I couldn't help noticing Deloris. She was always happy and cheerful—seemed like no matter what was going on she always had a smile on her face. Only today she looked right serious. The corners of her mouth were curved down, and she kept nibbling on her bottom lip.

Mama bowed her head and we all held hands around the table. Daddy didn't say grace. I lifted my head, just a tiny bit, and peeked at him out of one eye. He sat there, frowning at Mama. She didn't look up. Finally he blessed our meal and started passing the food.

I put roast beef, green beans, carrots, and a roll on my plate. I didn't eat anything, though. For a time I thought I was the only one not eating. Then I got to looking around. Kimmerly pitched in and already had gravy on her chin, but everybody else was just sort of sitting there. We looked—one to another—just waiting, wondering what was going on.

Daddy started eating just like nothing was the least bit unusual. The rest of us played with our food more than we ate. Daddy said as how the cotton crop was looking right good and how the calves up on the north section were fattening up just fine, only we probably needed to fix some fence on the east side of the pasture. Then he talked about the weather and how it was a mite cooler than it had been and if we got another rain how we might get one more hay cutting. Then, just as matter of fact as if he was talking about the weather, he asked Mama why she had the four big steamer trunks.

"Packing some things," Mama answered, hardly looking up from the butter she was spreading on her roll.

"Gonna store some old stuff in the barn?"

"Nope." Mama shook her head and chewed a bite off her roll.

Daddy cleared his throat.

"Hauling some of the kids' old clothes off to the neighbors?"

Mama shook her head and pointed to her mouth. She was all the time getting onto us kids for talking with something in our mouths. She was letting Daddy know she was eating and couldn't answer.

Daddy cocked his head way to one side. I could see his cheek bulge when his tongue traced a little circle around the inside of his mouth.

"Just exactly what and why are you packing?"

Mama swallowed her bite of roll and dabbed her mouth with a napkin. She smiled.

"I'm packing clothes and household things, mostly. The kids and I are moving."

I felt like somebody whacked me betwixt the eyes with an oak log. My head snapped back and I might near choked on the mouthful of green beans.

"Really?" Daddy looked down at his plate instead of at her.

"Really."

A silence hovered over the dinner table like a hawk hovering over a baby rabbit. I held my breath. The green beans I swallowed stuck in my throat as if they was fixing to choke me. Guess everybody else held their breath, too. It was so quiet I could hear Daddy's knife scratching his plate when he cut a piece of roast beef. Mama poured herself some tea from the pitcher. Daddy started to put the bite of roast to his mouth. About an inch or two from his lips, he stopped. Twirling the fork between his thumb and finger, he stared at the meat.

"Where might you be moving to?"

"Our place in Montana."

Daddy's eyes scrunched down tight.

"We don't have a ranch in Montana, remember? It got wiped out the winter of eighty-six."

"Not talking about the ranch." Mama was still calm and casual. "Our mountain valley place. The little cabin out west of the Flathead." She put some more butter on her roll. "I've always loved that valley. It's the most beautiful place I ever set eyes on. The air's clean and it's cool and . . ."

*"Cool?"*

Daddy sat at the head of our table. Mama sat clean at the other end. When Daddy said "Cool," it was more like he roared the word. He said it so loud that I almost felt the hair stand up on my head from the wind.

"Cool?" he repeated. "That's what this is about. Now, Ruth, I done told you that the heat sickness don't bother me no more. I'm over it. I feel just fine, so why don't you leave it be and . . ."

Suddenly Mama was on her feet. She leaned down the table and shook her finger right in Daddy's nose.

Mama never yelled. Even when she was getting ready to switch one of us boys for not minding, she never so much as raised her voice. But when she jumped up and shook her finger at Daddy, every glass on the table rattled when she roared, "Don't you lie to me, John Trumbull!"

I jumped back in my chair. My eyes felt as big around as saucers. Deloris jumped back, too. Kimmerly commenced to crying and climbed up in my lap.

"Don't even think about lying to me. I know about you throwing up down by the creek . . ."

Daddy's eyes shot to Daniel. Daniel ducked his head and chased his slice of roast beef from one side of his plate to the other with his fork.

"And I know about you falling down while you were cutting cedar fence posts up on the east hill."

Daddy glanced at Andrew, kind of twitched his mouth to the side, then turned again to glare at Daniel.

"Might as well quit bad-eyeing Daniel. Kimmerly was chasing crawdads and saw you. Andrew, Deloris, and me had to threaten Daniel with death 'fore he fessed up that you got too hot in the hayloft. He also told me you made him promise not to tell on you."

Daddy kind of flinched. He turned his glare from Daniel and onto Mama.

"Now, Ruth"—he tried to calm down—"I know you love the valley place in Montana. And I know we promised each other that when we got old and retired, we'd move back there someday. But I dang sure ain't old! And I'm not ready to quit farming! This place would fall apart if I wasn't around to—"

"Daniel and I can handle the place, just fine." Andrew didn't look up. Deloris reached out a trembling hand and held his.

Daddy gave a little snort and turned back to Mama.

"I'm not leaving my farm. You want to leave, you just go right ahead."

I was scared when the rattlesnake almost got me. I was even more scared when Kimmerly and I found Daddy in the cotton patch and thought he was dead. This kind of scare was different, but it was every bit as bad—maybe worse.

# CHAPTER 10

THE SCARED JUST WOULDN'T GO AWAY. Fact was, it kept getting worse and worse. My stomach felt like it had knots in it. I wanted to throw up or sit down and cry. But when you're eleven, a guy just doesn't bawl. Leastways, not around his older brothers. I saved my crying for night, when I was in my own bed.

It took Mama three days to pack. She left most of the kitchen things for Deloris and Esther. She did pack her favorite old black skillet and some pans. There was a cookie jar that her mother gave her and her good silver. The rest of the room in the four steamer trunks was for our clothes and bed linens and the like.

During that three days, Mama and Daddy didn't talk. Well, they did, but every time they started, they got to screaming at each other. Kimmerly would commence crying and crawl up in my lap. So they left their talking for outside—away from the house and away from us kids.

Kimmerly was a total pest. I could hardly get out of her reach. She spent a bunch of time hanging on to me. But, to be right honest, it helped me some. In a way, her little hugs felt kind of good. Lots of times I hugged her back. That felt good, too. I told her that everything was going to be all right. When I did, I tried so hard to convince her that I almost started believing it myself—almost, but not quite.

Early Wednesday morning Mama got Daniel and Andrew to load the steamer trunks on the spring wagon. She had us put on our Sunday-go-to-meeting clothes and our good shoes. Then she sent us to the wagon.

Kimmerly cried all the time Deloris was fixing her hair. I think Deloris cried, too. When Mama said it was time to go, Kimmerly hid under the kitchen table.

I wanted under there with her.

Mama fetched her out and dragged her by one arm to the wagon. With her bawling and kicking and flailing, I had a time holding her on my lap while Mama went back inside.

After a time she came out and stepped down from the dog-trot. Daddy stood at the door, watching her.

She stopped to look back at him. Then, in a real soft voice, she said, "John, I love you more than you'll ever know. I can't imagine being without you." Then her face got real stern and tight. "Fact is, I love you so much that I can't bare the thought of watching you kill yourself in this heat. Me and the kids are moving to Montana. We want you to come. We *need you.* I don't know if we can make it without you. But we're going!"

I just *thought* I was scared before. I don't remember being so scared about anything as when Mama said that and turned to climb up on the wagon seat. I wanted to cry. I wanted to jump down and wrap my arms around the horse's legs so they couldn't move. I wanted the whole world to quit rushing and spinning and I wanted things back the way they used to be.

My heart stopped when she took the reins from the dash.

"Ruth, wait!" Daddy called from the doorway. "You win!"

Reluctant for a moment, Mama finally climbed down from the wagon. The two of them went into the house. They stayed inside for what seemed like forever. I didn't know people could hold their breath forever. But I think that the whole bunch of us didn't breathe once, not all the time they were inside.

When they came back outside, neither were smiling. But they weren't glaring at each other, either. At least that was an improvement.

"We've reached a compromise," Daddy announced.

"Leave your things be and come inside," Mama said. "We need to have a family talk."

Excited, yet still awfully nervous, we climbed down and scurried to gather around the dinner table.

"What's a copper mine?" Kimmerly asked.

"A copper mine is where people mine for copper." I frowned down at her. "What Daddy said is that they've reached a *compromise.*"

Kimmerly frowned back. "What's a coppermize?"

"Compromise! Compromise. It's where two people agree on something. It's not really exactly what either of them wants—not altogether—but they're both kind of okay with it . . . sort of . . ."

The look on her face told me she still didn't understand. I really didn't either, so I stuck a finger to my lips and shushed her.

"Just hush up and listen."

All of us sat quietly at our places around the dinner table while Mama and Daddy explained what they had decided.

They had agreed that, when school was out in the spring, we would all move to Montana, together. They hadn't been to "their place" in the mountains for over twelve years. Daddy didn't even know if the cabin was still standing. They said we would have to build a new house, down in the valley. That was on account of the deep snows in the mountains would close the pass and us kids couldn't get to school. Luke said we didn't need to go to school. Mama and Daddy just ignored him. They told us that lots of work would need to be done and summer was the best time for us to make the move.

Daddy gave his word that he would mind Mama and do what Doc Harrison said. Mama gave her word that, if he didn't, we would move to Montana—right then and there. Daddy was a man of his word. There was no doubt in any of our minds that Mama was a woman of her word, too. Especially when it came to this.

Things got pretty much back to normal. It was great! Then again, it was kind of irritating, too. Seemed like a powerful long time that I worried about Mama and Daddy. Their fighting yanked knots in my stomach. I lay awake at nights, listening for them. I worried myself almost sick when they fought or when I thought about Mama taking us kids and leaving. Now they acted like nothing had happened—without so much as an "I'm sorry" to us kids.

Parents just ought not treat their kids that way.

School started in September. I liked being with Lester Franks and Scott McAtee. They were my best friends. Leastwise, they were my best friends until Emmerson Foster showed up. Then they'd scurry off to pretend they were playing somewhere else. When Emmerson was done pestering me or calling me a coward or trying to pick a fight, Lester and Scott came back. Guess they didn't want Emmerson picking on them. They were my best friends, but even best friends will only stick with you so far. Guess they had to look out for themselves.

At home there were chores to do and plans to make for when we moved in the spring. Daddy wanted to build a log home. Mama wanted a two-story house, like ones they pictured in the Sears & Roebuck Catalogue. I didn't care what kind of house we had, just so long as they didn't start fighting about it. The thing I *did want* was to get away from Emmerson Foster. Leaving Lester and Scott behind . . . well, I didn't look forward to that. But just the thought of leaving Emmerson Foster behind—that made me smile every time I thought about it.

In November Daniel and Esther got married. It was a right nice thing and lots of people showed up. They went by train to Kansas City and spent a week for their honeymoon. In December I played one of the Wise Men in our school Christmas play. In February we celebrated the twins' birthday. Mama, Deloris, and Esther baked a huge cake and put on a feed. There was so much food it liked to made all of us sick. I would miss Andrew and Deloris and Daniel and Esther.

In March some men came down from Tulsa, up in the Oklahoma Territory, and talked with Daddy about drilling another oil well on our place. Daddy agreed and said as how, when he was a kid, the black stuff that oozed from the ground was nothing but a nuisance. It made the cows sick or killed them. They used to build fences around the black bog to keep the cattle out. He still couldn't believe that folks were willing to pay good money for oil.

In April our teacher, Mr. Buchannon, caught Emmerson Foster trying to pick a fight with me on the playground. Emmerson kept shoving me and threatening to punch me. Mr. Buchannon latched on to his ear and dragged him inside. As soon as the class was seated, he switched him good with the birch rod and told us there would be no fighting at his school.

Emmerson kept glaring at me every time Mr. Buchannon swatted him. When school let out, Mr. Buchannon was still keeping an eye on him. Emmerson smiled when he walked past me. "I'm gonna get you," he threatened. "One of these days, after school when he ain't watching, I'm gonna get you!"

I'd miss Scott and Lester. I hated leaving Andrew, Deloris, Daniel, and Esther. Just the thought of being without them made me sad.

School let out on May 30. The next day Daddy hauled the four steamer trunks from the barn and we started packing. The thought of not having to spend another Fourth of July with Emmerson Foster . . . well, it almost made me look forward to leaving my home for a new place.

I wouldn't miss Emmerson Foster—not one little bit!

# CHAPTER 11

ON JUNE FOURTH ANDREW, DANIEL, ESther, and Deloris drove us to the train depot in Abilene. We did a bunch of hugging and kissing and Mama even cried a bit, before we boarded.

I felt kind of mixed up inside. I was excited and anxious about moving to our new home. I'd never seen Montana, and from listening to Mama and Daddy talk, it was the most beautiful place on earth. Still, I sure knew that I would miss my two older brothers. It's right hard to be excited and sad—all at the same time. But that's how I felt.

The train took us clean across Texas, through grasslands that looked like I'd always pictured the ocean. Only this ocean, instead of being blue, was mile after mile of brown, waving grass. The train took us all the way to Santa Fe.

We spent the night in a Harvey House, right next to the train station. Mama and Kimmerly slept in a room. Daddy went with us boys up to "the commons" on the top floor. The commons was just a wide open room with beds all over the place. There were cowhands and peddlers and us. The next day Daddy paid the man and said "thank you."

Early that morning we caught the train that took us north. We rode in the passenger car. There weren't too many people, so Kimmerly got to run up and down the long aisle and work some of the wiggles out of her system. The wood benches were hard and uncomfortable. I even got up a few times and pretended to chase after her, just to get some of my kinks out. It made for a long day.

The night breeze coming through the windows was cool. The *clickity-clack* of the train wheels on the steel rails was comforting. Still, I felt all mixed up inside. I was glad to be away from Emmerson. But what would it be like without Andrew and Daniel? Would I have friends at our new home like I did back in Abilene? Were people pretty much the same in Montana as in Texas, or was it like moving to a whole new world?

I pondered on it some. I worried about it some. Between the thinking and riding the hard wood seats, I was plum tuckered. Anyhow, I'd just dozed off when Luke flicked me on the ear with his finger. I jumped and turned to glare back at him. From the wood bench behind where Matthew and I sat, he pointed out the window.

"What's that?" he whispered.

Frowning and still not really awake, I followed where his finger was aimed. In the distance, down in what kind of looked like a hollowed-out bowl, was a whole bunch of lights. It looked like hundreds of little fireflies, flickering and clumped together. My bottom hurt from all the time on the wood bench. I wiggled and leaned my head out the train window.

"Fireflies?" I asked more than answered him.

Daddy sat on the bench, in front of me, with Kimmerly. He glanced over his shoulder.

"Denver."

"What's Denver?" I whispered back.

"It's a big city. The lights you're seein' are streetlights."

"You mean gas lamps like back in Abilene?" Patrick asked.

Daddy shook his head.

"Electric lights," Daddy answered. "The whole town is lit up with them. They burn all night long."

It was right pretty. The sparkle and glow seemed to flicker in the night, bringing life to the dark. We watched the lights clear into the train station.

At the depot some men set our steamer trunks on a Pullman cart. Daddy went inside while we stayed with our things. When he came back, he told Patrick that our next train wouldn't leave until ten in the morning. Then Daddy whispered something to Mama. She nodded and whispered something back. Then Daddy pulled Patrick aside and Mama turned to us.

"We have something we need to do. You kids stay here and watch our stuff. Mind Patrick. And *all of you* watch Kimmerly. We'll be back."

With that, both of them walked away. Frowning and puzzled, we watched them go. The second they were out of sight, we jumped Patrick.

"What did they say?"

"Where are they going?"

"Are they having another fight?"

"What's going on?"

Patrick just shook his head and waved for us to be quiet. "Y'all shut up! They got something they need to tend to. They'll be back."

An eternity passed. Our train pulled in. Mama and Daddy still weren't back. The porter looked at the tag on our steamer trunks, and some men started loading them on the train. Mama and Daddy still weren't back. I fidgeted, looked all around, wondering what could have happened to them. The men put our trunks in the baggage car. Mama and Daddy still weren't back.

Now I was getting scared.

They finally got there about five minutes before the porter yelled: "All aboard!" Both of them carried a package wrapped with brown paper and tied up with a bright ribbon. No matter how much we pestered, they wouldn't tell us where they went or what was in the packages.

About noon we teetered and balanced our way to the dining car. It was a fancy thing with bright brass chandeliers and lace tablecloths. The glasses on the tables made a right pretty little "tink" sound if something bumped them. Mama and Daddy took the packages with them. About the time we were finishing up our meal, a man with a tall, floppy white hat came to our table. With a big smile, he set a cake in front of us. It had five candles on it.

My heart sank clear down into my stomach. I wished Kimmerly Happy Birthday, just like the rest of my family—but even while I was saying it, I felt downright rotten inside. I couldn't believe I forgot her birthday. I hadn't even given it a thought. She was my only sister and I didn't even remember her fifth birthday.

Mama handed her one of the packages. Kimmerly ripped the brown paper to shreds getting into it. There were two dresses inside. One a bright blue and the other white. Mama told her the white one was from Matthew and Luke. The blue one was from Patrick and me. Then Daddy handed her the other package. It was smaller. He told her that this one was from all of us.

Kimmerly loved the little china doll. It had a

painted face and hands that were made of bright, shiny hard china. The body was cloth and her dress was almost the same color blue as the dress that Mama and Daddy told Kimmerly that Patrick and I got her. Only, I didn't get her a dress. I didn't even think about her birthday.

Kimmerly hugged and kissed and played with her doll all the way across Colorado and part of Wyoming. We slept and when we woke the next morning, the sun was up and the mountains were all around us.

The train clung to the edge of the cliff. Out the right side there was nothing but a sheer rock wall and a few pine trees. Out the left side there was a canyon. Down at the bottom was a little stream that was as clear and glimmering as our spring back home. Only instead of just sitting there, the water rushed and bubbled over rocks as it tumbled its way along.

It was right pretty as were the tall pine trees that loomed above it on the other side of the canyon. We came to a big, wide valley. Daddy said it was the Flathead. There was a lake out the left side of the train. But I'd never seen a lake like that. The thing was huge! The water was as smooth as a looking glass. I could see every cloud and every mountain and every tree looking back at me from the surface of that lake.

Reckon it was about the prettiest, most peaceful thing I ever saw. The beauty of it made me smile. But every time I smiled, I thought about Kimmerly.

She was such a sweet little thing. She never hurt anybody or picked a fuss. All she wanted to do was hug and snuggle and give those little wet, sloppy kisses.

I didn't know if the guilt about forgetting her birthday would ever go away.

# CHAPTER 12

IT WAS AFTERNOON WHEN WE PULLED INTO Kalispell.

"Place is a whole lot different from the last time we were here," Daddy said.

"I wonder if Jack Demers' General Store is still around," Mama asked.

A porter, with his striped hat and blue suit, pulled the big Pullman cart along with our trunks.

"Jack Demers moved his store from Head of Navigation, back in ninety-two," he told Mama. "Now, instead of down on the lake, it's about three blocks from here. On Main Street, right across from the courthouse."

"What's Head of Navigation?" I whispered.

Nobody answered.

"Nothing here but an empty field," Daddy marveled. "Wonder why Jack up and moved?"

"What's Head of Navigation?" I asked a little louder this time.

"Railhead came." The porter answered Daddy, not me. "Didn't take old Jack long to figure it was cheaper to ship supplies by rail than the old paddleboat what run up the lake from Polson. When he moved the store, what few people were around, well, they up and moved, too. A bunch more keep coming and coming. Don't slow down pretty soon, Kalispell's gonna be as big as Denver."

I stopped and tugged on Mama's skirt. "What's Head of Navigation?"

She motioned toward the river with a jerk of her head. "It's the pier down on the lake, where the river flows into it. It's where the steamships used to dock. They called it Head of Navigation because it's up here on this end of the lake or at the headwaters."

I kind of shrugged and nodded my head. Not that I knew much more than I did when I started, but at least *somebody* finally took the time to answer me.

We spent another night in a hotel. Daddy said it was about twelve to fifteen miles to "their place," and we would start early tomorrow morning.

As always, Daddy was up before first light. I heard him stirring, but wrapped the blanket around my head and went right back to sleep.

By eight he was back with a team and wagon he bought at the livery. He also made a stop for supplies at Jack Demers' store. We drove the wagon through a little park, and across a brand spanking new steel bridge over the Flathead River. From there we headed north on the Columbia Falls Stage Road. It was still morning when we got to Columbia Falls. Mama and Daddy marveled at how different the little town was. They said that there was no sawmill here before, and they didn't remember the wood lot.

From Columbia Falls, we followed the river for only a half mile or so, then turned north. We followed a logging road. Least, that's what Daddy said it was. He could tell on account of it was so well traveled and the wagon ruts were so deep.

"Must be cutting a powerful lot of timber up in the mountains," he said.

Six miles or so from Columbia Falls, we turned left and drove the team up a hill. It was so steep that everybody but Daddy got out. Patrick, Matthew, Luke, and I helped push the wagon.

Once to the top of the ridge, there was a flat area. Off to the right were a couple of ponds. Only they weren't brown and muddy, like the cow tanks back home. These were clear and so still and bright that it reminded me of Flathead Lake. These were a lot smaller, but I could still see every little cloud in the sky reflected on their surface.

Daddy stopped the team so they could drink and rest. We kind of leaned on the wagon wheels to catch our breath, too. Kimmerly trotted off to inspect the first pond. Mama followed after her.

"Right pretty little ponds," I panted from where I leaned over the tailboard. "Lots of flowers around them, too."

"Big one's called Spoon Lake." Daddy laced the reins around the brake-bar and hopped down. "Spoon was your mother's maiden name, 'fore we got married."

"What's the other one?" I sucked in a deep breath.

Daddy watched Mama and Kimmerly scampering through the field. Kimmerly was grabbing some of the wildflowers. He sighed and glanced back at me.

"Huh?"

"The little pond," I repeated. "It got a name?"

Daddy looked at me. He frowned, tilted his head to one side, then smiled.

"Reckon we'll just call it Bailey Lake. You think that's a good name for it?"

I smiled back at him.

"Yes, sir. Bailey Lake is a right good name for it."

The smile stuck to my face like honey sticks to a sweet roll. It clung there when Kimmerly brought back an armload of wildflowers and stuck them in my nose. It stayed there, stretching my ears, while we drove the wagon through a narrow canyon where we had to chop small trees and move logs to get through. We followed another little creek to the right and started up a steep grade. It was hard pushing the wagon. I was still smiling, though.

About halfway up the hill the road cut back sharp to the left. I looked down and we were right on the edge. We inched our way along for another hundred yards or so, when Daddy stopped the team and set the brake.

"Road's washed out," he called. "We'll have to pack in from here."

We unloaded the wagon and unhooked the team. It took all of us, even Mama and Kimmerly, to roll the wagon back down the edge of the cliff to a place where it was wide enough to turn it around. There wasn't hardly room to turn the horses, so Daddy backed them down. We took their harnesses off and tied the long, driving reins to a tree—giving them plenty of slack to graze.

Even after all the hard work of unloading and backing the wagon, I was still smiling like an egg-suckin' dog. Even if it was a small lake, it was *my* lake. It had *my name.* Don't reckon just anybody gets a lake named after them. It even made my chest puff up.

When we walked back up the trail to our steamer trunks, Daddy stopped. He seemed to study them for a moment before he turned to Mama.

"You pack my rifle?"

Mama pointed. "In that first trunk, there."

Daddy opened it. Took his rifle out.

"Think we'll leave the trunks here, for now." He cocked the lever-action and peeked to make sure it was loaded. "We'll come back for them if the cabin is still standing and in good enough shape to spend the night."

Daddy led the way.

"What's the rifle for?" Luke asked Patrick.

"Grizzly bear, mountain lion, wolves." Patrick had his eyes on the path and didn't even bother to glance back.

Luke stopped so quick that Matthew bumped into the back of him.

"You're kidding."

Patrick just kept walking.

"Nope."

Luke and Matthew just looked at him with their mouths flopped open. I scooted around in front of them.

"Fella back in Kalispell told me that trappers had taken all the wolves for their pelts," Daddy called from the front of the line. "Said there were still plenty of bear around. Sometimes they'll move into an old abandoned cabin. Make the thing their winter home. Don't hurt to be too careful around grizz."

The smile got tugged off my face for just an instant. The thought of bears and wolves and mountain lions kind of sent the hair prickling on the back of my neck and started me looking around.

But the smile came right back.

The steep walk and the thin air up in the high mountains left all of us huffing and puffing. That proud smile stayed with me, though.

Until I saw the cabin.

Our new home was a total wreck!

The cabin was made of logs with a split-shingle roof. Only, half of the roof had caved in. The swing-latch door lay on the ground, and two of the window shutters were off. Grass and wildflowers had grown up around the thing, as high as my knees.

From what little I could see, inside of the cabin was even worse.

Daddy told us to stay out in the yard. He clutched his rifle in his hand. It led the way as he walked, slow and cautiouslike toward the cabin.

A smell came to me. I couldn't quite figure what it was. The muscles in my face pinched my nose shut, then opened when I sucked another deep breath.

It was a bad smell. But there was something familiar about the odor. Where . . . what . . . I couldn't figure. Something back in Abilene. A smell I knew, but . . .

From out in the basin or meadow, I could see a little ways inside. There was a bed, but the mattress stuffing was torn and scattered about the room. There were sticks and limbs and twigs cluttering the place.

What was that smell?

Suddenly every muscle in my body sprang tight

and taut. In my mind's eye I could see the old medicine man who told fortunes at the Fourth of July sideshow, back in Abilene.

*"You will see yourself in the eye of the great bear,"* he had said.

I saw myself standing near the cage where the old black bear was. Waiting with the crowd of people. Hoping he would open his eyes so I could see myself.

That was the smell!

It was a . . .

"BEAR!"

I screamed the word at the top of my lungs. I grabbed for Mama's arm.

It was too late. Daddy had already disappeared inside the cabin.

# CHAPTER 13

"BEAR?" DADDY YELPED.

He came flying out from the cabin. He had his rifle to his shoulder.

"Bear? What bear? Where?"

"In the cabin," I shrieked.

He spun. Then slowly he turned back toward us. His face was all crinkled up—frowning, snearing, confused. The rifle sagged from his shoulder to dangle at his side.

"There's no bear in there."

"Yeah, there is. I smelled it. I know that smell. It's . . . it's . . ."

"It's raccoons." Daddy gave me a long, hard look. He shook his head and motioned back at the cabin with the barrel of his rifle.

"Just raccoons."

"You sure?" Mama called.

"Raccoons," he repeated.

My shoulders sagged. The air *whooshed* out of my chest.

"Looks like two families. One in the chimney and the other living in the old dresser. It's a real mess."

Mama brushed past me. "Bear," she said and gave a little snort. "Bailey, don't scare me like that." Then to the others, "Come on, kids. Sounds like we got our work cut out for us."

Patrick glared at me when he walked past.

"Bear," he muttered.

"Idiot," Matthew scoffed when he bumped my shoulder on his way to follow Mama.

Luke sneered at me and called me a knot-head. Kimmerly just smiled and went into the cabin.

Talk about feeling like a fool . . .

I was so embarrassed, I couldn't even face them. I stood outside the cabin for a time, shifting from one foot to the other. When I finally got up the nerve to go in, they were coming out.

We brought the tools up first. At the general store, Daddy had bought a couple of axes, a froe (for splitting shingles), an auger and bits, two saws, two shovels, two hammers, rope, some hinges, and a broom. After that was at the cabin, we went back for the steamer trunks.

The high mountain air was thin and hard to breathe.

It seemed to make even little chores, like walking, next to impossible.

Mama and Daddy carried stuff out of the cabin. Mama swept while Daddy fixed the doors and shutters. The door was still solid and in good shape, only the leather strap-hinges had torn off. He whittled wood pegs, used the auger to bore holes, and set the door with steel hinges. Then he did the same with the shutters.

Next, he and the twins started chopping wood to fix the roof. He handed Patrick and me shovels and told us to go fill in the road where it had washed out, so we could get the team and wagon up the hill.

I used to think that chopping cotton was hard work. By the time Patrick and I shoveled enough dirt to repair the washout in the road, I felt like we must have moved a whole mountain. It was almost dark by the time we were done and had the horses to the house.

We were so busy working, I hadn't had time to look over our new place. We were up high, but there weren't many trees—just a few small pines sprinkled around. Our little basin was mostly grass and wildflowers. There was a creek running through it and high, rocky peaks on three sides. Out front of the cabin, the land dropped away toward the Flathead, but there were so many big trees at the far edge and on the next ridge, I couldn't see much else.

Before the light was all gone, we all marched to a

place on the creek to wash for supper. The place we stopped looked just like our spring, back in Texas. There was a small, round pool for drinking water, a larger pool below it for bathing, and another pool below that for Mama to do her laundry. The water was as clear and fresh as back home. The only difference was . . .

COLD!

I never knew water could be so cold. Even in the wintertime back home, our spring was warmer than this creek. When it was real cold, we hauled buckets of water to the house and bathed in a big tub in the middle of the floor. This stuff was like bathing in ice water.

It didn't take any of us long to wash up. I could hear my teeth chattering when we headed back to the cabin.

Reckon the whole family was just as wore out as Patrick and I were. Daddy and the twins had done a lot, but there was still a sizable hole left in the roof. Mama had cleaned and swept the whole cabin by herself. Kimmerly spent most of her time chasing butterflies or picking wildflowers. When we got to the cabin, Mama dug around in one of the sacks Daddy brought from the general store. It was kind of neat to unwrap paper and find bread already sliced into thin pieces. In another sack she found meat that was already cooked. We ate, then dug our bed stuff from the trunks. We laid them in a neat row near the fireplace and dived in.

Yes, sir. I sure was going to sleep good tonight.

Right about the time I thought that—right as I was snuggled into my bedroll and starting to relax—that's when the *real* work started.

Daddy called it a dispute over territory. I called it an out-and-out battle royal.

Seems like the raccoons had no respect for the fact that Daddy built the cabin with his own two hands. Nor did they consider that the whole family (except for Kimmerly) had been working all day to clean up their mess. They didn't care, in the least, that we were plum tuckered.

The raccoons wanted their house.

We wanted *our* house.

There was definitely a problem.

I was almost asleep when I heard a scratching sound. Then there was sort of a chattering, followed by more scratching. The chattering opened one of my eyes. It didn't stay open. I smushed the pillow around my ears and went back to sleep. Then there was a snort. A sound kind of like a pig makes when he's playing in the mud. It was followed by more chattering and scratching.

The snort opened both my eyes.

"Afraid of that," Daddy mumbled.

I went right back to sleep, only I didn't stay asleep

very long. Next thing I heard was Daddy yelling and Mama whacking and pounding her pillow on the wood floor. I sat straight up in my bedroll. There was some light coming through the big hole in the roof. In the dim shadows from the half moon, I could see Daddy kicking at something near the fireplace. Mama came at the fireplace, too, swinging her pillow.

The whole bunch of us stayed sitting up while Daddy went outside and fetched in some wood. In the big fireplace he piled small kindling pieces on the bottom and bigger sticks on the top. He lit the pile then crawled back in his bedroll.

"I'll get up a couple of times during the night," he said with a sigh. "Keep it going so the 'coons won't crawl down the chimney, but keep it small enough so it doesn't burn us out."

Far as I was concerned, there was no worry about burning us out. Once finished shoveling a whole mountain to fill in the washout in the road, I got downright cold. My bedroll was a sheet and two blankets. One blanket was for laying on, the other for wrapping up. I already had both blankets bunched around me. And right before I dozed off, I'd seriously thought of trying to snitch Matthew's blanket.

Just the glow of the fire seemed to warm the room. I lay back down and closed my eyes. Sleep came quick and sweet.

The scream was loud enough to wake the dead.

# CHAPTER 14

I SAT STRAIGHT UP WITH BOTH FISTS clinched in front of my lap and ready to fight. At the sound of the second scream, I kicked the sheet and blankets off.

"Luke!" Daddy yelled. "Luke, what's wrong?"

Then a third scream came.

"Matthew?" Mama called.

There was more screaming and thrashing around and kicking and hollering. My legs took over, like always. Before I knew it, I was standing on the fireplace hearth with my back pressed against the rock. Kimmerly was up there with me. She had both arms wrapped around my legs. I hugged her back. With everybody else leaping and scurrying about the cabin, it was hard to make out what was happening. Daddy was suddenly beside us. He reached into the fire and found a limb that was burning only on one end. He held it up like a torch. The glow filled the cabin.

Before my eyes could adjust and make out what was happening, there was a loud *crash!*

Daddy rushed toward the sound. Calm as could be, Mama walked to the door. She flung it open and stepped aside.

A big, fuzzy animal—about the size of a large watermelon—flew outside through the door. Another animal followed. It was a raccoon, all hunkered up and fuzzed. I could hear them chattering at each other outside the cabin. The sound of their voices faded quickly into the night.

Then the screams filled my ears again.

"Lord help me! I'm sorry! Lord help me! I'll never do it again! I swear . . ."

Daddy knelt down. When his torch neared the ground, I could see a hole in our wood floor. He reached in, got hold of something and pulled. Arm first, Matthew appeared. Daddy lifted him clean up in the air and set him on one of the empty bedrolls. The second he touched the ground, Matthew's legs folded in under him. He crumpled there, whimpering and crying.

Mama went outside and brought back a couple of armloads of dry grass. Daddy tossed that, his torch, and some more wood on the fire. Light filled the cabin. Mama got everybody over beside the fireplace and started trying to sort stuff out.

It took some doing.

Seems like Luke woke up with a boar 'coon sitting square in the middle of his chest. When he opened his eyes and saw the thing staring at him and breathing on his face—he screamed. Reckon anybody would have. Only, when he screamed, the 'coon took off straight across his brother. Mama had Matthew lean down, closer to the fire. There were four little scratch marks right in the middle of his forehead.

Anyhow, Luke kept screaming. When the raccoon scratched Matthew, he jumped out of his bedroll. But when he got to his feet, he must have stepped on the smaller raccoon. Being sound asleep and suddenly finding himself on something warm and fuzzy and wiggly . . . well—he jumped. When he came down, he lit on some rotted boards under the hole in the roof. They snapped and he went right through the floor.

That's when he woke up. But when he woke up, he wasn't in the cabin with his family. He was down in a dark hole in the ground and he couldn't get out! Every time he tried to raise up, he hit one of the floorboards.

"What was all that 'Lord help me' and 'I'll never do it again', stuff?" Patrick sort of chuckled.

Matthew glared at him.

"You been doing something you're feeling guilty about?" Daddy teased.

Matthew glared at him, too.

"I thought I was dead," Matthew finally admitted. "I didn't know where I was, but it weren't where I wanted to be. And . . . and I didn't know what I had done wrong to get there, so I figured I'd . . . well, whatever it was, I . . . I thought it best to say I was sorry for it and . . . and, well . . ."

Everybody but Matthew thought it was funny. I couldn't help but notice how his hands and legs kept shaking. Even though he smiled with our laughing and teasing, he didn't see much humor in it.

The next day we finished repairing the roof. I got down in the floor and ripped out all the rotted boards, and we patched it, too. Sure enough, the raccoons came back. We could hear them scratching on the roof and chattering to one another. Patrick stayed out there until about midnight or so, then Matthew took his place. Four hours later it was my turn.

I just felt like I got to sleep when somebody started shaking me. I grunted and rolled over. Luke shoved me hard.

"Get up," he whispered. "It's your turn to chase the 'coons."

I wrapped the pillow around my head. He shoved me so hard, I bumped into Matthew. Matthew shoved me back. Rolled me so hard that I clunked into Luke again.

"All right. All right, I'm up."

I gathered my pillow and bedroll and staggered out

the door. Daddy had built a ladder out of logs and rope. It was leaned against the side of the cabin. Still half asleep, I waddled to it, climbed to the roof, and spread out my stuff.

I'd never noticed what a steep pitch the roof had, not until I put my things down and they started sliding off. I ended up sitting on my pillow at the very tip-top of the cabin. I wrapped the sheet and blankets around me to keep from freezing to death.

Even feeling miserable and surly, I had to admit I'd never seen such a sky full of stars before.

Reckon it had something to do with being up high in the mountains. They were so bright and sparkling that they seemed to dance in the sky. They twinkled and shimmered, almost close enough to touch. I knew good and well I couldn't. I stuck out a hand anyway and pretended to grab one. It made me smile.

It was a little before first light when I finally got comfortable. I found I could lay on my side with my elbow wrapped over the ridge of the roof. That way I didn't slide. The night was clear and there wasn't a breath of air moving. I never heard such stillness—never knew the world could be so quiet or so beautiful. That's when the door creaked.

"Bailey? Bailey, I gotta go potty."

Kimmerly's voice startled me. I raised my head and looked down at her between my bare feet.

Only when I lifted my head, I started to slide. I slipped faster and faster. Quick as a cat, I flipped over and grabbed for the shingles at the tip of the roof. Fingertips caught, just in the nick of time. In that second or two I guess I got going pretty fast. My fingers jerked me to a stop, but the blankets, sheet, and pillow kept sliding. I stretched and caught the ridge of shingles with my other hand. Straining, I pulled myself up until I could wrap my elbows over the top of the roof. I squirmed and twisted until I had my balance and could turn to get my bottom under me.

Kimmerly was out in the middle of the front yard. My pillow and the blankets were wadded up on the ground, but the sheet must have landed smack on top of her. All covered in white, she was flailing her arms and jumping around, trying to get the thing off. Kimmerly looked like a ghost at one of our Halloween parties at school.

A sly smile curled my lips when I thought how startled one of my brothers would be if they walked out of the house with her jumping around under that sheet. With my hands and feet under me, I lifted my bottom off the slick shingles and worked my way down to the ladder. Kimmerly had the sheet off by the time I got to the ground. She stood there, glaring at me.

"That was not nice, Bailey!"

I almost laughed at the mean look on her face.

"I didn't do it on purpose, Kimmerly. It slipped."

"It was a dirty trick."

"Oh, shush. You're gonna wake everybody up."

Her bottom lip stuck out.

I motioned toward the trees. "Thought you had to go potty. Go on."

"Come with me."

"I can see you from here."

Her bottom lip pouched out farther.

"It's scary by myself. Go with me."

My eyes rolled. I shook my head and got her hand.

"All right. Come on."

# CHAPTER 15

THE OUTHOUSE WAS IN A CLUMP OF TREES east of the cabin. Right now it wasn't really an outhouse. Except for the two-holer seat, the entire thing had tilted over and fallen apart. Hidden from the house by some little pine trees, and seeing as how there was nobody but family around for miles and miles . . . well, it really didn't matter.

On the way down the hill Kimmerly had a hundred questions, like: "Why is that flower blue?" "Why is that one yellow?" "Why is this place called a basin?" "What's a basin?" and on and on and on.

Mostly I ignored her or simply answered, "Because" or "I don't know." It didn't keep her from jabbering and asking even more questions.

I waited outside the clump of pines while she took care of her business. I kept watch on the cabin, hoping Mama would come out and I could dump Kimmerly on her. I wanted to explore this place and see what was here.

What would it be like come winter, up here? Would I have fun being in this new place, or would I hate it? Would the kids at school be the same as back home or . . .

All of a sudden there were a million and one questions floating around inside my head and . . .

"Bailey? The paper's wet."

"Open the catalog and get a dry page from inside."

"Okay."

And a million and one things to see and places to explore and no time to . . .

"Thank you, Bailey."

"You're welcome. Now hurry up."

And no time to explore it. If I just had a couple of hours to myself . . .

"I got to wash my hands."

"Well, come on."

Soon as Mama and Daddy got up, I'd ask them. No! I'd *tell* them that I needed somebody else to watch Kimmerly.

Come breakfast, Kimmerly was still hanging on to me and still jabbering. Mama handed out the last of the elk roast Daddy had bought in Kalispell. The elk was right good. But that's all we had to eat for two straight days. Even something good as elk roast, bread, and butter gets tiresome after two days. Daddy said grace and we pitched in. All of us except for Mama.

"We need to stock in some groceries," she began. "We're running short on . . ."

"What's a gosees?"

"Groceries," I corrected Kimmerly. "Just hush a minute and listen."

"But, Bailey," Kimmerly tugged on my shirtsleeve so hard that my hand dipped into the butter I just put on my bread. "What's groceries?"

"You know, supplies. Food and stuff," I snarled in a whisper. "You know good and well what groceries are, now hush."

"And your father and I want you to go with us," Mama went on.

"We need to decide on a building site for the new house," Daddy said. "We don't want it down in the bottom on the Flathead. But we can't stay here in the mountains. We have to find a location where there's not so much snow."

"What's a location?"

I ignored her.

"Your dad and I love this place. But come the winter snows . . ."

"Bailey, when does winter come?"

I put my finger against her lips and shushed her once more.

"If it were just the two of us—there's no place on earth we'd rather spend the rest of our days."

Daddy swallowed his bite of roast and nodded his agreement.

"Trouble is," he added, "come November or December, the pass up here—fact, this whole basin—is gonna be filled with snow. If it were just your mom and me, that wouldn't be so bad, but . . ."

"What's a basin?"

"Hush up, Kimmerly." I leaned down so I could stare eye to eye with her. "Don't interrupt."

"You kids have to be able to get to school and back. Besides that . . ."

"What's a basin?"

"Kimmerly!"

Mama reached over, took Kimmerly, and put her in her lap. She told her that a basin was sort of a bowl or low spot. We called this place a basin because it was a low meadow that was almost surrounded by mountains. Then she peeled the crust off her sandwich and made Kimmerly take a bite. Wished I'd thought of sticking food in Kimmerly's mouth. One way to keep her shut up.

"Last time I spent a winter here," Daddy continued, "there was better than twenty foot of snow on the pass. Figure that's why the thing washed out. Too much snow. Patrick and Bailey fixed the road and we can get the wagon through, but come winter we'll be snowed in."

"Why is it a basin instead of a valley? A valley has mountains around it."

"A valley is long and narrow. The basin is more round. Here. Take another bite of your breakfast."

"What your mother and I have decided is that . . ."

"What's the name of our basin?" Kimmerly got up on her knees and leaned way out over the table.

I thought about swatting her bottom. But Daddy stopped talking and looked at her. Mama stopped trying to set her back down and looked at Daddy. Then both of them sort of smiled at each other.

"Reckon it ought to have a name," Daddy said to Mama.

She winked and kind of nodded toward Kimmerly.

"Why not?" Daddy shrugged.

"What's the name of our basin?" Kimmerly repeated.

"Kimmerly Basin." They both answered her at the same time.

Kimmerly's eyes lit up like Fourth of July skyrockets.

"Really?"

"Really. Now sit down and be quiet. What your father has to say is important and it's for all of us. You're gonna sit and be still for a while so we can all hear."

The look Mama gave Kimmerly shut her up.

Daddy commenced to talking—only I wasn't listening. Not at first, anyway.

It's right strange, the way a boy's mind works.

I heard what Daddy was saying. I heard him tell us that we would all decide on a place for the house. It would have to be near the logging road we came up here on, so us kids could get to school in Columbia Falls. While we were in town for supplies, he would find a couple of men to help us with the work. He said that he also planned to have Andrew ship a few head of cattle up for us to raise.

Daddy said that he figured we'd be so busy with the house and building the fence, we wouldn't have time to cut firewood. Besides that, he liked the heat that oak and hickory gave off better than burning pine. So, we would have Andrew contact the Carlisle brothers, up by Baird, and have them ship a boxcar load of firewood when Andrew sent the cattle.

I listened and heard all that, but at the same time I heard it, my head and my feelings were racing about Kimmerly Basin.

It made me mad. I was so proud when Daddy named the little lake Bailey Lake. But it was just a little puddle. It didn't matter that Daddy called it a lake. Shoot, back home it wouldn't even be big enough to call a stock tank. But this place . . .

It was "their place." It was Mama's and Daddy's favorite spot in the whole entire world. They stayed here when they first got married. When they had the big cattle ranch out east of the mountains, they left it with their foreman, every summer, and came to spend a couple of weeks at "their place." Even after the bad winter of 1886, when they lost everything and had to move back to Abilene, they still talked about "their place" in the mountains.

Now "their place" had a name. It was Kimmerly Basin.

It hurt my feelings that they named a little puddle after me, but their favorite place in the whole wide world—they named Kimmerly Basin.

Then, still listening to what they were saying and still feeling mad at Kimmerly for being their "favorite" and still feeling sorry for myself . . . I got mad!

Only, I wasn't mad at Kimmerly. And I wasn't mad at Mama and Daddy. I was mad at me!

Kimmerly was my sister. I shouldn't feel jealous about them naming "their place" Kimmerly Basin. I shouldn't be jealous—only I was. That's what made me mad. That, and maybe just a little feeling inside that they loved Kimmerly more than they did me. Only I knew it was wrong to feel that way. But . . .

The thoughts came flying at me so fast and hard that my head couldn't keep it straight. It was like a whirlwind. Mama and Daddy and my brothers were all talking, but my head was going a hundred times faster than their words.

*Slow down!* I screamed at myself inside my head.

*Don't think bad stuff about your baby sister! Think something good!*

The smile made my jaw relax. It made my teeth quit grinding together. The smile felt good.

*I'll never have to spend another Fourth of July with Emmerson Foster throwing firecrackers at me.*

My tongue traced a little circle around my lips, and my smile grew and grew.

# CHAPTER 16

WE SPENT THE NEXT THREE WEEKS AT THE cabin in Kimmerly Basin. Each morning Daddy, Patrick, Luke, Matthew, and I hopped in the wagon and drove down the hill to work on our new house. Sometimes Mama and Kimmerly went with us. Other times they stayed at the cabin and fixed food for the next day. Well, Mama fixed food. Kimmerly spent most of her time picking wildflowers.

The spot we picked for our new home was on a flat, level piece of land just up the hill from Spoon Lake and Bailey Lake.

Daddy hired two young men to help. We cut trees, dragged them to the house with the two-horse team, peeled the bark, and notched them. When all that was done, we rolled them into place for the walls. As soon as we had the roof on the thing, Daddy said it was time to move down the mountain.

On July 3 we didn't have to work on the house. That morning we packed up all our stuff and loaded it on the wagon. By ten o'clock everything was ready for the move.

Everything but Kimmerly.

Like usual, she was no place to be found.

"Bailey, go find Kimmerly."

That was the story of my life—go find Kimmerly. It took a while, but I finally located her in the outhouse. We had rebuilt the thing, and even when I called her, she didn't answer. I found her, hunkered up in the corner with her arms wrapped around her knees.

"What's wrong, Kimmerly?" I growled, still irritated that she hadn't answered when I called.

She sniffed and looked up at me.

"I dropped my dolly."

I glanced down at the two-holer seat. My nose crinkled up. There was no way I was fishing that doll out of . . .

"A big raccoon scared me and I dropped my dolly."

My shoulders sagged, relieved that the doll wasn't down there in all that stuff. I took her arm and yanked her outside.

"Raccoon ain't gonna hurt you. Quit acting like a baby and show me where you left your doll."

"But it was big, Bailey. It was a giant raccoon. *HUGE!*"

I just shook my head and dragged her around the side of the outhouse. We found her doll. "See. No giant raccoon. Now, get to the wagon." I pointed her in the right direction and gave her a swat on the bottom to send her on her way. She was so happy to get "dolly" back, she didn't even tattle to Mama about me swatting her.

We slept downstairs on our bedrolls. I had a heck of a time getting to sleep. I was so excited about tomorrow, I couldn't seem to relax. The thought of having a Fourth of July without Emmerson Foster around to pester me . . . well, I don't think I got a wink of sleep, all night.

The BANG was so loud, I couldn't help myself.

I jumped!

It wasn't like I'd never heard a firecracker before. After all, this was the big Fourth of July celebration. Seeing as how it was the turn of the century to boot, most folks in a fifty-mile radius had come to Kalispell for the goings-on. All the families had kids, and mite near all the boys had firecrackers. The blamed things had been going off since first light.

But this one sounded like a gunshot. It exploded so close to my right foot that sparks and dirt stung the bare skin as if it were on fire.

Like I said, I couldn't help myself. I jumped. Guess most anybody would.

But unlike most anybody, when I jumped—I JUMPED.

In my head I knew it was a stupid thing to do. In my head I could see Emmerson Foster and his gang of guys. In my head I knew it was going to start all over again.

I knew all that stuff—in my head. My brain told me not to jump. Not to run. Trouble was, my feet just flat wouldn't listen.

I came clean off the ground, probably so high that the bottoms of my bare feet were where my belt was just a second before. Then when I lit, I hopped again. Not once or twice, but about three or four times.

There were nearly five seconds of silence. The only sound I could hear was my heart thumping in my head. Then the laughter started.

A little giggle, a chuckle at first. Only it grew and grew until the laughter around me sounded more like a roar.

There were probably fifteen or so boys hanging around the park just southeast of the Kalispell courthouse. But their laughter was so loud it sounded like twice that many.

"Never seen nobody jump like that," a voice came from the crowd.

"Squealed like a little girl," another added.

Inside my head I could hear my teeth grinding together. My fists clinched at my side. No matter what, I told myself, *don't jump.* Don't even move!

"Shoot," a redheaded kid in bib overalls scoffed. "My sister don't even jump and squeal like that. Ain't never seen the like."

Sure enough . . .

I heard the hiss. From the corner of my eye, I caught the smoke puff. Little red and orange sparks fizzed from the tip of the fuse. It spun and tumbled over and over when it flew through the air.

The *POP* came before it even touched the ground beside me. And at the exact same second the *BANG* sounded, my feet left the ground. The instant they came down, I hopped again and again and again. These hops, instead of being in place, carried me away from the direction of the firecracker.

I felt a sinking feeling in my chest. I knew good and well what would happen next.

Sure enough, this time two hisses came from my other side. I was in the air *before* the pops.

Next thing I knew, I was running. Bare feet pounded the ground. My head and feet weren't even connected. My head told me to stop! Turn and face them. Fight if you have to!

My feet just ran—not paying the least bit of attention to my head.

I raced through the park, dodged one tree, then another. A young couple had a picnic dinner spread on a blanket. I jumped clean over it. The man yelled at me. A couple of seconds later, I could hear him yell at the boys who were chasing me.

They were gaining.

I ran around the edge of the courthouse and headed up Main Street. The laughter behind me sounded like a pack of coyotes yapping at a jackrabbit. I hated feeling like a rabbit.

I hated feeling like a *coward!*

Firecrackers popped, but they weren't even close. I broke stride, just long enough to glance back over a shoulder. There were only six boys following me. I turned left and darted across the street.

The man driving a four-passenger surrey with his family had to yank the reins to keep his horse from hitting me. I made it but didn't even see the team and six-passenger rockaway coming from the other direction. I slid to a stop to keep from hitting the wagon.

The *POP* was a lot closer this time.

"Don't be throwin' them things around the horses!" the man on the rockaway yelled at the boys behind me. "Blamed idiots gonna get somebody hurt. I ought to climb down off'n this wagon and give you a good switchin'. Get on outa here or . . ."

I didn't hear what else he had to say. The firecracker was close enough that my feet took over once more.

I ran about two blocks, then darted to my left and raced through an alley. When I came out onto a different street, I turned left again. A sign about half-way down the block said DEMERS GENERAL STORE. Panting and out of breath, I slipped inside.

"Help you, son?" a friendly voice called.

I looked around and saw a plump man in a white shirt and apron behind the counter. Another man stood there, talking with him.

"No, thank you, sir." I kind of held my breath so he wouldn't hear me gasping for air. "Just looking around."

He gave me sort of a suspicious look, then smiled. "Make yourself to home. You need any help, I'll be with you soon as I take care of Mr. Decker, here." He smiled and went back to visiting with the man.

Pretending to look at shirts and shoes, I moved around so I had a tall counter between me and the front window. Sure enough, it wasn't more than a minute or two before the six boys came running down the street, hunting for me. I squatted so only my eyes were showing over the stacks of shirts.

I must have stayed in Demers General Store for twenty minutes or so, making sure the gang of boys had gone. I bought a penny sack of hard candy and headed off to find Mama and Daddy.

Here I was, almost two thousand miles from home, and darned if Emmerson Foster hadn't shown up to make my life miserable.

Well, he didn't look like Emmerson. This kid was short and had red hair instead of being tall with brown hair. I'd be willing to bet money that his name wasn't Emmerson Foster, either.

But it *was* Emmerson Foster, all right. Different look. Different name. It was still the same, still somebody calling me sissy and coward. Still the same laughing and pestering and making my life miserable.

Folks had come from all over for the big turn-of-the-century Independence Day celebration. Shoot, with any luck, I'd never even see that kid again.

# CHAPTER 17

"GOT NO IDEA WHO HE IS," DADDY grunted when I asked him about the redheaded boy in bib overalls. Course, the way he was straining and struggling with the crank on the ice-cream freezer, I wasn't even sure he was paying that much attention to me. "Don't have the slightest idea. Here." He tapped the side of the wood-slat barrel with his left hand. "Latch on to this thing. Let me see if I can crank with both hands."

I knelt on one knee in front of him and got hold of the barrel. Daddy put both hands on the crank. Even with me hanging on hard as I could, he might near knocked me over when he started turning it.

"From Bailey's description, sounds like Johnny Carver," Grady Buffalo said. Grady sat, cranking his ice-cream freezer, on the wood bench just to the right of Daddy. He was full-blood Flathead and was one of Daddy's hired hands. Austin Davis sat on Daddy's left. His folks were Texans, like us, but he was born and raised here in Montana. He leaned around Daddy and looked at Grady.

"Johnny? Isn't he Benjamin's kid, over to the sawmill?"

Grady leaned forward. He kind of had to bob back and forth to see Austin. That was because Daddy was between them, rocking to and fro as he fought with the handle on the ice-cream freezer.

"Sounds like him, all right. Did he have a shirt on under his overalls?"

I shook my head.

"No."

Grady and Austin nodded.

"That's Johnny Carver. Kid hardly ever wears a shirt under his overalls, not even in the wintertime."

"You're talking about the sawmill here in Kalispell?" I said it almost praying instead of asking.

"No." Austin bit down on his lip and twisted his ice-cream freezer so he could get a better grip on it. "The sawmill up in Columbia Falls."

"Where we live? Where we'll be going to school?"

Grady and Austin nodded again. "Think he's about twelve or so," Grady said. "Same age as you, Bailey. You two will probably be in the same class. Why do you ask?"

My heart sank clean down into my bare feet, then

oozed out into the dirt. I wanted to curl up and die. I couldn't even answer. All I could do was shake my head.

Grady held his ice-cream freezer between his feet and scratched his chin with his free hand. He shrugged, then looked over at me. Grady's soft smile always made me feel good.

"Do best not to run with him," he said. "Old man Carver's a pretty nice fella, but I've heard my younger brother talk about Johnny. He's kind of an ill-tempered, nasty little kid. Always trying to bully the boys at school and stuff like that."

Daddy gave one final crank that liked to jerked me off my knee. He stopped and wiped the sweat from his forehead with his shirtsleeve.

"This batch is done. Fetch it to your mother and tell her I'm all cranked out. You crank the next batch, Bailey."

I picked up the wood ice-cream freezer and weaved my way between all the people who showed up for the Fourth of July church social. Mama stood with some other women behind a long serving table. It was covered with a red-checkered cloth. The women dipped ice cream from the freezers and served up cakes and pies that they brought from home as people came through the line.

I wanted to tell her about the boys chasing me with firecrackers—just like back in Abilene. I wanted to tell her how horrible it was to find out that I was going be stuck at the same school with Johnny Carver. I wanted to tell her how he sounded and acted just exactly like Emmerson Foster.

Thing was, there were more pressing matters at hand.

I started to heave the ice-cream freezer onto the table beside her. With a jerk of her head, she motioned to the row of freezers sitting on a blanket behind the serving tables. I gave a grunt when I lifted it, then set it down in line with the others. I walked back to her.

"Daddy's sweating," I announced.

Mama frowned.

"Is he bad?"

I shrugged. "Told me I'd have to crank the next batch. Said he was plum tuckered out."

Mama let go of the big wood serving spoon. It tilted forward and sank into the soft ice cream—real slow—like a log sinking in quicksand. She looked around. Patrick was standing not far away talking with a tall, skinny young lady in a taffeta dress.

"Molly," Mama called.

The girl looked up. Her face flushed a little when she saw Mama watching her. Patrick's face turned bright red, too. He spun, pretending he wasn't really there, much less talking with a girl. Mama didn't pay them any mind.

"Molly," she repeated. "Could you come and take

my place here? I have something I need to attend to."

The girl scurried over beside Mama and took the spoon from the ice cream. A little boy in a blue shirt stood on the other side of the table. Barely tall enough to reach, he clunked his bowl a couple of times, impatient at having to wait. The young woman dug into the freezer and plopped a big spoonful of ice cream in his bowl. His face lit up with a smile that stretched from ear to ear.

Mama and I spun, taking off to where Daddy was, and almost ran over Patrick.

"Is it Daddy?"

"He's not bad." I held my hands up, trying to calm him.

Mama offered a gentle smile. "We're just going to check on him. You can stay here and help Molly."

Patrick stepped aside. "I'll be back in a second, Molly." He leaned around Mama to smile at the girl. "Don't run off."

Molly smiled back at him and fluttered her eyes. I looked up at Patrick and fluttered my eyes, just like she did. With a disgusted sneer, Patrick punched me on the shoulder. It wasn't a hard punch. I still said "Ouch" and commenced rubbing my arm.

"Where is he?" Patrick snapped.

I fought my way through the crowd of people with Patrick and Mama right behind me. I was sure Daddy was okay. I felt a little ashamed for worrying them so. Still, the memory of last summer lingered in my head. As we walked through all the people, I could almost see it in my mind's eye, just like it was happening again—right now.

Daddy was cool as a cucumber by the time we got back to him. Mama asked if he was okay. He shot me a look that kind of made me want to scrunch down and hide behind Mama. Then he smiled at her and said as how he was fine. His arm was all wore out from cranking the ice-cream freezer, on account of he was using different muscles than he did chopping logs for the house.

"Besides that, today's my birthday," he boasted. "All these people here for my celebration and I been doing nothing but making ice cream all day. Bailey can crank the next batch—not 'cause I'm too hot. I just wanna go eat something. Any of your cake left?"

Mama shook her head. "Sorry."

I nudged her with my shoulder. She shot me a look, almost as bad as the one Daddy gave me for telling Mama about him breaking a sweat. I knew she had a special cake with candles, just for his birthday. She didn't want Daddy to know and she didn't want me to so much as give the slightest hint about it. I hushed. Tried to figure some way to change the subject, real quick.

"Where's Kimmerly?"

"Think she's with the twins." Mama frowned. "Not

sure, though. Most times, Kimmerly's not where she's supposed to be."

Daddy made a grunting sound when he got up.

"I guess I'll go eat some other lady's cake," he mumbled, sounding right sorry for himself. "Patrick, why don't you crank the next freezer full of ice cream. Bailey, you go find Kimmerly."

Just my luck. I was looking forward to sitting down and visiting with Grady and Austin. They were right nice young men. Hard workers, they had a good sense of humor and were fun to talk with. Besides, if I stayed with them I wouldn't have to worry about bumping into Emmerson—I mean that redheaded kid with the bib overalls.

But, noooo. I had to go shoot my mouth off. I had to ask, "Where's Kimmerly?" Now I'd be the one stuck with her.

# CHAPTER 18

I WAS STUCK WITH KIMMERLY.

When Daddy had said, "Bailey, go find Kimmerly," it hadn't taken me long to locate her. She was at the Kalispell Park—clinging to the center pole on the little merry-go-round. She'd talked Luke and Matthew into letting her ride the thing, only some of the bigger boys had got to spinning it too fast and she got scared. Instead of prying her loose when she wouldn't let go of the center pole, the twins just up and left her. They went off someplace to play or shoot off firecrackers.

Kimmerly was the only one on the merry-go-round when I got there. But how many times she'd spun around or how many other kids had come and gone while she held her death grip on the pole, it was hard to tell.

Kimmerly was one pitiful-looking little creature. She was shaking and crying. I had to pry her fingers and arms from around the pole, then drag her off the thing. Her eyes were kind of glazed over and her face was as white as the new dress Mama had put on her this morning. When I tried to stand her up, I couldn't let go. Every time I did, she'd start staggering and tip over. As we headed back to find Mama and Daddy, she threw up. It got all over her Sunday-go-to-meetin' dress and her new white shoes.

Mama took her down by the river and got her all clean, while Daddy went to Demers General Store and got her a new dress. Soon as Kimmerly was all spiffied up, she latched on to my leg and wouldn't let go.

Thing I'd learned about the twins was you never took on just one twin. Matthew and Luke were as tight as jam and bread. You punched one, you best be ready to duck, 'cause the other would be coming at you quicker than you could blink. Even guys at school knew that. But it didn't matter—what they did to Kimmerly was wrong. They shouldn't have gone off and left her like that. I'd fight both of them. They were older and bigger—and there were two of them—it didn't matter. I'd still get in a couple of good punches before they took me down.

Thing was, Daddy saw them coming back to the wagon before I did. He was as calm as could be when he asked why they ran off and left their little sister. All they could do was hem and haw. Before they could think up a good excuse, he had his belt off and done had 'em switched.

Kimmerly hugged my leg so hard my foot almost went to sleep.

Patrick always said that Daddy could draw that belt faster than most gunfighters could draw their pistols. He'd always told me how lucky I was that Daddy had mellowed in his old age. He said that the twins and I didn't get near as many lickings as Andrew, Daniel, and he did when they were little.

After Luke and Matthew quit their crying, we went to watch the fireworks. Kimmerly sat next to me on the blanket and clung to my arm. They had these really neat things called Roman candles. Most of the men stood on the new steel railroad bridge over the Flathead River. When they lit the Roman candles, all these different colored balls came poofing out. Glowing fireballs of red, green, orange, or blue filled the night sky and reflected off the shimmering river. Men along the banks set off rockets.

All in all, it was the darndest Independence Day celebration I ever saw. Daddy said it was quite a show, too. But he said that it was only fitting, seeing as how this was the turn of the century. It was a special day—a special time. Most folks never get to see a whole century turn over. None of us would ever see another.

Kimmerly hung on to my hand while we walked back to the wagon. Once there, Mama sneaked Daddy's special birthday cake out from under the wagon seat. She lit the candles, and we all gathered around when she handed it to him.

Daddy was surprised!

Matthew, Luke, and I gave him a new pair of work gloves. He needed them right bad. Patrick gave him a pocketknife. It had two shiny blades and a white handle that shimmered in the light from our campfire. Patrick told him it was a pearl handle. It looked as bright and sparkly as new snow. Daddy was right proud of it. He was proud of the new gloves, too. The thing that really got him, though, was the present Mama and Kimmerly gave him.

Kimmerly had been hanging on to my shirttail or my leg ever since the fireworks started. She finally let go of me so she and Mama could go after his gift. It felt good to be loose from her for a moment. Mama told Daddy she had left his present with the people camped next to us, 'cause he was so snoopy she figured he might find it. They came back and Kimmerly handed him this long, skinny pole with a big round, silver-looking thing attached to the base of it.

The pole was a good nine foot long, and Kimmerly had trouble carrying it. Mama helped her. Daddy took it. Held it out in one hand to look it over.

"This is really nice." He smiled. "Wonderful present. Thank you, Kimmerly. Thank you, Ruth. I never had anything like it." He kept smiling all the time he was thanking them. Then when he was done, he kind of tilted his head to one side and frowned—studying the thing.

"What is it?" he finally asked Mama.

She laughed. "It's called a fly rod." She pointed to the round, silver thing with the little lever. "That's an automatic reel. Jack Demers says it's the best thing there is for fishing. You know, catching trout?"

Daddy's lip arched up on one side. Austin gave a little chuckle.

"They really are fun, Mr. Trumbull. My dad, brother, and me—all three of us got 'em. Ours aren't automatic, though. You got to turn the reel by hand."

"I have one, too," Grady said. "Dad doesn't believe in the things. Says you ought to catch fish the old way."

Daddy glanced at him and nodded. "Big rock or a sharp stick."

"Yes, sir," Grady agreed. "But Mom got me a fly rod and reel last Christmas. I always bring home more fish than Dad ever did. You get a trout on the end of that long rod . . . you never had such a fight . . ."

"Don't have to hide in the bushes or behind a big rock, neither," Austin sounded excited when he interrupted Grady. "You can get—"

"You can get right out in the stream with the fish," Grady jumped in when Austin took a breath.

I could hear the excitement every time Austin or Grady said something. They both wanted to talk at the same time and kept butting in whenever the other hesitated for so much as half a second.

Back in Texas we always went home as soon as the fireworks were over. For a time I figured we'd do the same. After all, it wasn't that far on the Columbia Falls Stage Road. But Daddy, Austin, and Grady kept talking way into the night. Patrick stayed up with them, but Mama put the rest of us to bed.

I had a right hard time getting to sleep. Seemed like every time I closed my eyes, that redheaded kid in the bib overalls was there. His beady eyes kept glaring at me and his jeering laughter filled my ears. I'd open my eyes, sit up in my bedroll, and shake him out of my head. But as soon as I lay back down again, Emmerson Foster was there.

Mama always said, "Things will be better in the morning." Between Emmerson Foster and Johnny Carver tormenting my dreams, I didn't think morning would ever come.

# CHAPTER 19

WHEN MORNING CAME, I THOUGHT WE'D head home at first light. It was well after noon when we finally hitched the wagon and headed to the house. That was because, first thing in the morning, Daddy and our two hired hands went fishing.

On the way out of town we stopped by Jack Demers' General Store. Daddy didn't tell us why. We just stopped.

Mama and Kimmerly went to look at some of the bolt goods. Daddy, Grady, and Austin went to look at dry flies. They told Daddy that tying his own flies was the best. But until he'd had some time to practice, he needed some store-bought ones. Mr. Demers greeted us and visited. I was off by myself, looking at a glass case with pocketknives in it, when I felt a hand on my shoulder.

"You finally shake that gang of boys who was chasing you yesterday?" Mr. Demers smiled.

I didn't think he knew I was hiding in his store yesterday. I thought I'd been sneaky enough about it that he didn't have the slightest idea. It was right surprising.

I swallowed and gave a quick nod. He glanced around to make sure nobody was listening. His smile was kind and easy.

"I know three of those boys. They're nothing but bullies. They run in a pack, kind of like wolves. Alone, they aren't tough at all. You don't need to run from 'em. You don't need to be scared of 'em."

I wanted to tell him I wasn't scared of them. I wanted to tell him how the firecrackers—the loud noise when I wasn't expecting it—that was what got me running. I wanted to tell him that I wasn't a coward.

My shoulders sagged and all I could do was smile up at him and nod. He went to help Daddy.

Mama almost died when we left Jack Demers General Store with six more fly rods, reels, and a whole basket full of flies. Daddy got her a bolt of blue print cotton. That quieted her, some. She still yammered at him most all the way home.

"Fishing by yourself is no fun," Daddy told her. "Soon as we're done with the house, I'm gonna take the whole family fishing. We might even go up in the high country—up by old man MacDonald's lake. Fish some of those cold streams by the glaciers."

Kimmerly was snuggled up against me in the back of the wagon. She sat up, then climbed over the seat to sit between Mama and Daddy. I was glad.

"What's a glacier?" she started in.

I had a right peaceful trip back home. Without Kimmerly clinging to me, I stretched out in the back of the wagon and took a nap—slept clean into Columbia Falls.

The stage road went right by the sawmill. I yawned and stretched, then pulled myself so I could see over the edge of the boards. There was always something going on at the sawmill—wagons coming and going, men carrying logs into the big building with the high roof, or men carrying lumber out to stack it in the sun.

When I sat up, I spotted three boys sitting on the roof of the mill house. Trouble was, one of them spotted me.

They were just sitting there, visiting. Suddenly this redheaded kid in bib overalls jumped. He scrambled to his feet and pointed. I slid back down into the bedrolls that were piled on the floor of the wagon. Through the cracks in the wood, I saw him slap his leg. I couldn't hear him from that far away, but I could see him laughing. The other boys stretched their necks. I pushed myself deeper into the pile of bedrolls.

I knew he was telling them about me. I knew he was telling how I took off running when they threw firecrackers. He was laughing about how they chased me all over town. He was probably telling them what a sissy I was—what a coward.

*I'm not a coward!* I snarled to myself.

But the second I told myself that, I saw me hiding in the pile of bedrolls—flattened down like a weasel hiding in a hollow log. I saw myself hiding behind Mama and Daddy and the boards of the wagon. I felt myself hoping and praying that the other two boys on the roof of the sawmill hadn't seen me.

Maybe he was right. Maybe I was a coward.

Over the next couple of weeks I tried to keep the thought pushed out of my head. It kept coming back. Even when we were working on the house and busy, this little, nagging voice inside my head kept saying: "Bailey Trumbull is a coward. Bailey Trumbull is a sissy. He ran clean to Montana, with his folks, to get away from boys who chase him and make fun of him. Even up here, he's still a coward!"

Every evening, before it got dark, the whole family went to the lakes to practice our fly-fishing. I liked that. But every night I thought about the redheaded boy in the bib overalls. And every morning, when I woke up, the thoughts—the little voices—they were still there gnawing at me.

We finished the house on July 27. Before supper we all gathered on the little hump between Spoon Lake and Bailey Lake to look at it from a distance.

Our house was one of the most beautiful homes I ever imagined. A two-story log cabin, it had a log porch and deck that went clean around three sides. The inside, except for the living room, was covered with tongue-n-grove boards, straight from the sawmill in Columbia Falls.

Each room had a window. Mama and Daddy could see the trees from their downstairs bedroom. Upstairs, Patrick and the twins had a view of the mountains out back of the house. From Kimmerly's bedroom, at the front of the upstairs, you could see across the valley—almost to the North Fork of the Flathead River. My window had the best view. I could look out and see *my* lake, clear and shimmering down in the open meadow. It was right pretty, what with the wildflowers growing in the meadow around Bailey Lake and over the little hump toward Spoon Lake.

Leastways, there used to be wildflowers.

Kimmerly brought in an armload of flowers one morning before breakfast. Mama put them in a vase and really made over them, telling Kimmerly how beautiful the flowers looked on the dining table. Ever since then, Kimmerly went out of a morning and fetched Mama fresh flowers for her table. Between her picking flowers and us tromping them down while we were practicing our fly-fishing each evening before dark, there was hardly a flower left on the whole place.

After we looked at the house and kind of patted ourselves on the backs for what a good job we had done, we went inside for supper. Daddy said grace, but before he started passing the food, he kind of cleared his throat and sat up real straight in his chair.

"We've worked hard," he announced. "Figure we deserve a good week of fishing up in the high country."

Grady, Austin, and all the rest of us nodded our agreement.

"Day after tomorrow, we're headed out to see if we can't catch some fish." Daddy smiled and started passing the food.

Austin took the deviled eggs from him and put a couple on his plate. "You sure set a right fine table, Mrs. Trumbull."

"Right pretty," Grady agreed.

"Thank you." Mama smiled. Then she turned to frown at Daddy. "Day after tomorrow is Sunday. We'll miss church."

Next to me, I heard Kimmerly sniff. Daddy made a growling sound when he cleared his throat.

"Don't think the good Lord is gonna hold one Sunday against us." He was smiling when he said it, but his voice was serious and so was the look he gave Mama. "Besides, a fella don't never feel closer to God as when he's up in the high country. There's just something about the mountains and the trees and . . ."

Kimmerly sniffed again. It was louder this time. So loud that I quit listening to Daddy and glanced over at her. She had tears leaking from her eyes. One of them dripped into her green beans.

"Kimmerly, what's the matter?" I whispered.

"Mama's table ain't pretty," she sobbed. "It don't have no pretty flowers. How can it be pretty without flowers?"

"He was just talking. It's pretty on account of she fixes such good food and has her dishes and all. It was a compliment. You know—to make her feel good."

"But Mama says the flowers are pretty. I can't find flowers. They're all gone."

Daddy leaned toward us. Guess we had been whispering louder than I thought. "Kimmerly, don't you go frettin' about flowers. There's lots of flowers up where we're going."

Her eyes kind of lit up.

"Really?"

"Sure," Patrick jumped in. "Remember all the flowers up at Kimmerly Basin? Where we're going is even higher than that. Got even more flowers. You can pick all the flowers you want."

When Kimmerly quit her sniffing and blubbering, everybody went back to talking about fishing and what we needed to pack and all that stuff.

Kimmerly kind of gazed off at the ceiling, like she was thinking on something. Her tears dried and a smile stretched her red cheeks.

Nobody thought another thing about it. After all, Kimmerly was just a little kid. Five-year-olds think kind of weird—I mean, making such a big fuss over her mama not having flowers on the table. It was silly.

We all got caught up in the excitement of the big trip and didn't give Kimmerly another thought. Not until . . .

# CHAPTER 20

KIMMERLY WAS THERE AT BREAKFAST, ALL smiling and happy. Soon as breakfast was done, Mama and Daddy hitched two of our horses to the wagon and headed to the general store in Columbia Falls. Mama needed supplies to take on our trip, and Daddy needed to pick up some barbed wire. The firewood that the Carlisle brothers were cutting for us, back in Abilene, and our cattle were due to arrive in about two weeks. Daddy wanted everything ready so we could start building fence when we got back from the high country.

Us boys stayed home to pack. Daddy said we'd need warm clothes, at least a couple pairs of Levi's and an extra pair of shoes. Only extra shoes I had were school shoes from year before last. They hurt my feet, but they'd be okay for tromping through a cold stream and fishing.

Around noon I glanced out the bedroom window and saw the team and wagon coming up the hill. I grabbed two more shirts and stuffed them into the bag I was packing. When I looked out again, the team and wagon were out front of the house.

"Kids, come here!" Daddy yelled from the foot of the stairs. He waited a moment, while we all gathered at the top of the steps. "We've had a little change in plans," he announced. "We're gonna go ahead and leave now, instead of waiting until morning, and . . ." He stopped, sort of frowning.

"Kimmerly," he called. "Get on out here. You need to hear this, too."

We waited. Patrick turned toward her room and cupped his hand along the side of his mouth. He took a deep breath, like he was fixing to yell at her. Suddenly his hand dropped to his side and he looked down at Daddy.

"She went with you and Mama, didn't she?"

The twins and I nodded our agreement.

Daddy glanced at Mama, then frowned back up at us.

"No. She stayed here with you boys, to pack."

Shaking our heads, we frowned at one another. Patrick darted into Kimmerly's room. Mama headed to the kitchen. In a matter of seconds, both of them came back. I couldn't help notice the worried look on Mama's face.

"Not there," they echoed at the same time.

Daddy's deep voice rumbled through the house: "All right, let's find her!"

Just like Kimmerly, I thought. Never where she's supposed to be. Everybody started calling her name. Luke and Matthew checked the rooms upstairs. Daddy went through the downstairs. I headed to the back, to go look in the outhouse. Mama was already there, peeking through the door by the time I got down the steps. She saw me and shook her head.

"I'll look in the barn," I called. "See if Austin or Grady have seen her."

For the next ten minutes all of us were combing the whole place. We could hear each other calling Kimmerly's name. But there was no answer.

A shrill, high-pitched whistle cut the air. Daddy could put his little fingers against the corners of his mouth and whistle real loud. I never learned how. This whistle was so loud and piercing, it cut through the spruce and fir and pine like a bullet shooting through a paper target. I felt the little smile tug at the corners of my mouth. Someone must have found her and Daddy was calling us in.

Daddy and Mama were standing about halfway between the house and the barn. Kimmerly wasn't with them.

When we all got there, Daddy cleared his throat. "Okay. She just must have wandered out of earshot. Let's get the horses. We can cover more ground that way." He took a deep breath and cleared his throat again. "Grady, you head north. Austin, south. Patrick east, and . . . Matthew, you go west."

We all spun and headed for the pen out beside the barn.

"Which way do I go, Daddy?" Luke asked.

"Take the logging road toward Columbia Falls. I'm pretty sure your mom and I would have spotted her when we came back from town. But just to make sure . . ."

"How about me?"

Daddy laid a big, callused hand on my shoulder. I could feel him trembling.

"Bailey . . . ah . . . you take the logging road up north of the house. I'll go check the lakes."

"I'll go with you," Mama told him.

Suddenly Daddy stopped. He looked at her and shook his head. "No. I'll go alone."

I didn't understand why Daddy's face turned kind of pale. But when I looked at Mama, her face was just as white. Her eyes tightened.

"I'll go with you!" she repeated.

A chill shot through me. Bailey Lake . . . Spoon Lake. Kimmerly out there, all by herself. Us boys knew how to swim. But Kimmerly . . .

I swallowed down the knot in my throat and chased the thought away. Daddy gave me a little pat on the shoulder. I spun and took off.

When we moved to Montana from Texas, Daddy bought five horses and a wagon at the livery in Kalispell. He said we only needed two for the wagon, but come September and time for us to get the six miles down to school in Columbia Falls—we'd need them. With five horses there just wasn't enough to go around. Being the youngest, I figured I'd be the one on foot. So I just took off without even waiting for a horse.

I trotted across the flat, around the house, and down the hill. Just like her, I thought. Kimmerly is never where she's supposed to be. Here we are, ready to go on our big fishing trip, and we got to hunt for her.

It irritated me—but only for a split second. Then I got to thinking about Mama and Daddy going to the lakes, and a knot kind of lumped up in my throat. I trotted a little faster.

The logging road was down the hill from our house. I remembered that when we first came here last summer, it was hard to tell that it *was* a road. It was just a little path, barely wide enough to get our team and wagon through. Now that the sawmill had started logging up the Flathead River from us, the thing was like a highway. There were always wagons coming or going. Couple of times I had watched out Kimmerly's window. Sometimes there were huge freight wagons with six to eight oxen pulling a big stack of enormous logs. Other times I'd seen teams of four to six mules or horses pulling smaller loads. The road was wide and the ruts were deep. Running on the patch of grass between the ruts, I could make good time.

I ran a ways, stopped, and called Kimmerly's name. When there was no answer, I ran on.

Not more than a mile from the house, I spotted a six-horse team and wagon coming toward me. I yelled Kimmerly's name one more time, then raced for the wagon.

An old man with a beard pulled the team up as I neared. One of the lead horses shied when I ran past.

"Did you see a little girl, back up the road there?" I asked, panting.

The old man pursed his lips and shook his head.

"Ain't seen a single soul for the last seven miles or so. Why?"

Even though I was panting for breath, my shoulders still sagged.

"We can't find my little sister. Looked all over the home place for her. She's probably playing somewheres. You sure you didn't see nobody?"

Again the old man shook his head. "Team's pulling slow today. Got plenty of time to look around. Only thing back up the road was three deer, one elk, and an old bull moose. Just caught sight of his rump going over the hill, yonder." The old man pointed.

I followed his finger. Frowned.

"What's up there?"

"Nothing much"—he shrugged—"just hills and mountains and trees—like everywhere else 'round here." He pointed again. "Take that back. There is a little log cabin, back in there a ways. Sets in this little basin at the edge of the Smoky Range. Don't think nobody lives there. Don't even think it's got a name."

Smiling, I recognized his description.

"It's got a name. It's called Kimmerly Basin."

The instant the words came out of my mouth, I jerked. It was like a little streak of lightning smacked me right between the shoulder blades. It was so sharp and hurtful that it seemed like somebody stabbed me with a knife.

In that same instant I remembered Kimmerly crying last night because Mama didn't have flowers for her table. And I remembered Patrick telling her how, when we went fishing up in the high country, there would be lots of flowers—*just like up in Kimmerly Basin.*

And—I knew where my little sister was.

# CHAPTER 21

QUICK AS A CAT, I LIFTED THE LONG, DRIVing reins with my left hand and hopped over the doubletree between the horses and wagon. I hit the ground running.

"Hey, boy!" a voice yelled behind me. "Boy, hold up!"

My feet slid in the dirt. Irritated at being slowed down, I glanced over my shoulder.

"I think I know where my sister is. I gotta go!"

"Wait up, boy." He climbed down from the wagon. I turned, but I was still leaning toward the hill. The old man frowned.

"You're one of John Trumbull's boys, aren't you?"

"Yes, sir."

"Where do you think your sister is?"

"Up at Kimmerly Basin." I pointed. "I just know

she's there. Daddy named that little basin you were talking about after her. She's finding flowers for Mama."

He studied me a minute. Deep canyons furrowed in his brow. "How old is your sister?"

"She's only five. I really got to go, mister."

"You try to go straight through, on foot, it'd take you all day. Land's too rough up there—too many mountains and gorges. Help me unhitch the lead team. We'll swing back by where your dad's building the new house and follow the creek. Be there in less than half an hour."

Mama and Daddy were still at Bailey Lake when we got there. It made me feel better. While I was helping the old man unhitch the team, a picture flashed through my mind's eye. For just an instant I could see Kimmerly, floating facedown . . .

Even now, when I think about it—the picture makes me shudder.

We pulled our horses up, not far from where they were.

"You find her?" Daddy called.

I shook my head.

"She's not here. Lakes are clear as a bell today. No tracks around the edge, either. Can't figure, for the life of me, where that child could . . ."

"I think I know," I said, cutting him off. "I think she's up at Kimmerly Basin. Remember—last night when she got to crying about the flowers? I just know she's up there."

Daddy slapped his leg. "Danged if I bet you ain't right. You two head on up there. Soon as one of the boys gets back with a horse, I'll follow along."

The old man next to me leaned down and reached out a hand.

"Ed Haskill." He shook Daddy's hand. "Met you and the missus about two weeks ago at the sawmill."

Daddy nodded. "I remember. Had a pretty nice visit. You still working there?"

"Driving a log wagon." He patted his horse on the rump. "No sense waiting for someone to ride in. This old horse can carry double. Come on."

He reached out. Daddy grabbed his arm and jumped. Mr. Haskill pulled. Slick as a whistle Daddy was sitting behind him on the horse.

We weren't even out of sight of Mama and Bailey Lake when I heard Mr. Haskill hollering behind me, "Dig your heels into that old horse, son. He hasn't been working that hard. Ought to be able to carry you at a gallop, clean up where we're headed."

I did like I was told. Three miles up the creek, the old horse was all lathered up and huffin' and puffin'. I stopped him, just short of the water. That's where the trail split. The left side went on up into the mountains. The creek crossing, to the right, was the trail up to Kimmerly Basin. I slid down from his back and looked around. There were shod hoof tracks following the left side of the creek. I didn't remember if it was Austin or Grady who Daddy sent this way. Whoever, they weren't headed for Kimmerly Basin. I took Mr. Haskill's horse to the stream and let him drink and cool down some. We moved on at a walk. When I heard Daddy and Mr. Haskill coming up behind me, I stopped again.

"Who come this way?" I called.

"Grady!" Daddy yelled back. "He go up to the basin?"

"No. Tracks are still following the creek. Want me to wait on you?"

"Go ahead," Mr. Haskill called. "Gonna let the horse drink and walk him a ways. We'll be along."

I didn't push my horse after we left the creek. The climb was a lot steeper here. We followed the wagon tracks we left while we stayed at the cabin. Grass was already starting to cover them. It was surprising how quick it took back over. We'd only moved down to the new house a couple of months ago, and the forest was already starting to cover our tracks.

Not far from the basin—where the road started switching back and forth for the steep climb—I pulled my horse up.

We spent one full day, working with shovels and dragging rocks, to fill the spot where the road had washed out. Now it was washed out again. All that hard work, just swished down the hill by a couple of heavy rains we had after we moved into the new house. I tried to rein my horse around the washout. The ground was loose and he slipped. We backed up and tried it again. This time he balked and didn't want to go on.

I slid off his back and wrapped the long driving reins around a little spruce tree.

"Stay here, you old knothead," I snarled at him. "Daddy's gonna give Kimmerly a good paddling for running off. Hope he switches you, too, for not minding me."

The horse just flipped his tail.

I looked at the road with the big washed-out trench that cut across it. I looked up. The hill was a steep climb, but it would be a lot quicker on foot. Using my hands to grab small fir trees and sagebrush, I headed straight up.

Below me, I could hear voices. It sounded like more than Mr. Haskill and Daddy, but I couldn't see on account of all the spruce, pine, and aspen were so thick. Climbing with my hands to pull and my feet digging and sliding on the loose mountain dirt, I fought my way to the first place where the road cut back. But instead of following it to the right, I just kept climbing.

I didn't even think about how steep the climb was until I stopped at the edge of Kimmerly Basin to catch my breath. Once on flat ground, I straightened up and looked back where I'd been. Sure glad I didn't slip, I thought with a smile. Would have ended up clean down at the bottom of the mountain.

Below me, Daddy and Mr. Haskill had tied their horse next to where I left mine. Following the road instead of climbing the mountain, they were only to the first switchback. Grady was down there, too. I caught a glimpse of him when he tied his horse, hopped the washed-out place in the road, and trotted to catch up with Daddy and Mr. Haskill.

Once I was breathing easier and feeling better, I followed the road over a little rise. From there I could see the whole basin. Kimmerly was no place in sight. I looked around. There weren't as many flowers as I thought—just a patch of blue and yellow out to the right side of the cabin. The patch seemed bigger back behind, but I couldn't tell for sure.

*I bet the little stink is back there,* I thought, glaring at the flowers. *And if Daddy don't switch her for running off and scaring us—I'm going to. There's no sense in her being so spoiled.*

The thought hadn't even cleared my head, when I heard the scream!

It was a high, shrill scream that pierced the air like an arrow. It sent the chills racing up my back.

In a second I saw her come tearing around the side of the cabin. She was running fast—headed straight down the wagon road toward me. For an instant I kind of smiled. I never knew her little, pudgy legs could move that fast. The smile didn't stay on my face for long.

Kimmerly screamed again.

Then I heard the roar!

It was a deep, bellowing sound—so low and horrible that it seemed to rattle the pine needles. It was so loud, the sound stayed in the basin forever as it bounced and echoed from the sheer rock cliffs.

Then I saw the bear.

He charged into sight from behind the cabin. It wasn't a bear like the one I saw at the sideshow back in Abilene. He wasn't black and sleepy with dull eyes. This bear was *huge!* He was brown colored with a patch of white running down his back.

Even from here, I could see his bright, glaring eyes. They were on Kimmerly—hot and intense. Slobbers flew from his mouth as he ran. He was chasing my little sister. Like a freight train roaring down a mountain, every crashing, lumbering stride brought him closer.

Kimmerly was halfway across the meadow and running hard by the time the bear came into sight. I knew she'd never make it to me.

The sound—the roar—it scared me. I wasn't expecting it. The sight of the enormous, angry bear . . . It scared me. I never saw anything so big and fierce and terrifying in my life. And just like always . . .

My feet took over. I ran.

# CHAPTER 22

IT WAS JUST LIKE ALWAYS. IT WAS LIKE MY feet had a mind all their own, and my head couldn't do one single thing to control them.

My head told me to run. Go get Daddy! Get Grady and the old man! Get up a tree! Run away!

My feet carried me across the basin, toward Kimmerly.

The bear was closer, now. He was less than a hundred yards away when I reached her and he was still gaining ground. There was no time to grab her and run. He was too close.

Kimmerly reached out to me as she ran. Guess she wanted me to pick her up—save her from the huge beast.

"NO!" I screamed. "NO! Run to Daddy! Down the hill. Run to Daddy!"

I pointed behind me and kept running.

For the first time in her life, Kimmerly minded me. She shot past on my left. I ran about ten more feet, then stopped. I glanced over my shoulder. She was still running, lickety-split toward where Daddy and the others were coming up the hill.

I turned to face the bear.

He was still thirty yards away. Even from this distance, his brown eyes looked as big around as my fists. He was looking right past me—still intent on Kimmerly.

I glanced over my shoulder to see where she was. I stepped to the side. Put myself right between her and the bear. Now he had to look at me. He had to see me instead of my little sister.

I closed my eyes and sucked in a deep breath. It would be the last breath I ever took.

I raised my arms and at the top of my lungs, I screamed, "NOOooooo! You leave her alone!"

When I opened my eyes, the whole world had changed. The bear was still charging. He was closing the short distance between us as fast as a hummingbird's wings beat the air. Only my eyes and my head took it all in like everything was slowed down.

I could see every little detail of each little second—no, each split second. And I could see it as clear and slow as could be.

I saw each drop of slobber that flew from his huge

white fangs. Each spatter of foam that sprayed back from his mouth to stick to his fur. It moved as slowly as a snail crawling across a rock.

Just as slow, I saw when his huge paws stretched out in front of him. I saw the long, sharp claws bury into the loose mountain dirt. I saw every little hair ripple above the strong muscles on his shoulders as he slid to a stop, right in front of me.

The dust swirled. The brown dirt puffed as slow as clouds crawling across a Texas sky. For a while he was gone, hidden behind the rolling clump of dust. The while was only a second or two. It seemed like forever.

Then he appeared again. He raised up on his hind legs. He kept going up and up and up, until he was towering above me—and the cloud of dust—like the mountains tower above the trees.

He roared.

I saw his long teeth—white with yellow around the bases. Pink gums and a darker tongue that looked like sandpaper. He raised a paw. It was as big around as my head. Long curved claws stuck out from the gray-brown pads. The paw bobbed up and down in the air.

He roared again.

The sound was so loud, it hurt my ears. It seemed to shake my chest. I felt his breath against my face.

Everything told me to run. My head—my legs—even my feet. One swipe from those enormous claws would rip me to shreds. His mouth could swallow my whole head with one bite. His teeth could rip me apart.

But something inside of me sort of snapped. It wasn't my feet. They didn't take over like always. It wasn't my head, either. Something deeper—something way down inside. I don't know where it came from or what it was.

I didn't move an inch. I just glared up at him and roared back, "You leave my sister alone!"

The giant bear tilted his head to one side. His black nostrils flared with a *whoompf* sound. His left paw bobbing up and down in the air like a wave, he roared again. For only an instant I glared back at him—stared him square in the eye.

And in that instant, I saw a twelve-year-old boy standing there. He stood with this arms stretched wide, as if he were foolish enough to think he could tackle this enormous beast if he tried to get past. He stood there on rubber legs that were shaking and wanting to run. He had tears in his eyes and one that rolled down his cheek because he wanted his mama and daddy, but he knew he'd never see his family again. Then I saw my eyes. It wasn't like a reflection—not like seeing into Mother's looking glass—it was as if I watched my own eyes, staring back at me. I can't explain it. I can't tell why. It just was. But those eyes wouldn't blink. They wouldn't run. They just stared.

The instant lasted for just a heartbeat. Then the bear roared again. I didn't roar back. My voice was soft and it didn't quiver.

"Go on and get out of here. She's my sister. You can't have her!"

He only stood there. He stood there for probably what was only two seconds, but what felt like two hours. And just as fast as he had rushed toward me—but what felt like just as slow—he dropped to all fours. He turned and walked back across the meadow.

I didn't move.

He disappeared behind our cabin.

I didn't move.

The last I saw of him, he vanished over a high ridge in the mountains that surrounded Kimmerly Basin.

He was gone.

It was over.

# CHAPTER 23

I DO REMEMBER DADDY COMING UP AND getting hold of my shoulders. I don't recollect walking down the hill to the horses. I do recall that nobody talked on the ride back from Kimmerly Basin to our house. Nobody said so much as a single word. And I remember seeing Kimmerly with her legs wrapped around Mama and her arms hugging her neck so tight Mama's face almost turned white, only I don't recall how she got off the horse or up in Mama's arms.

It was like there was kind of a haze or mist that covered the whole world. Like nothing was real and it was all something seen in a dream.

I know that everybody was there when we got back. There was even a couple of men I didn't know. I found out later that they were log drivers, like Mr.

Haskill. They'd spotted his rig on the road and come to see what was wrong. And I know, when I finally sort of woke up, or came back to the real world, we were all sitting in the living room—but I don't remember getting there or smelling the coffee Mama fixed, or hardly much else.

The first thing I really heard was Mr. Haskill's voice. He was talking to Austin.

"It wasn't a female, protecting a cub. Thing was a male. Full growed. Bet he was nine foot tall. Silver-back. Never seen a bear that big in all the fifty-four years I've been up here."

One of the other men spoke up. I didn't know who he was, but he had white hair and a salt-and-pepper beard, sort of like Mr. Haskill's.

"Every year some family or some logger finds remains. Figure there's maybe four or five folks a year lost to bear, up in this country."

Mr. Haskill nodded.

"Everyone I ever heard of what run onto a grizzly got torn to shreds or kilt and eaten. In all my years, I never seen the like of what I witnessed today."

"The Flathead got a legend about it." I recognized Grady's voice. "I just thought it was talk. You know, stories about the old days, folktales, and the like. My grandfather told it. He said that once every three generations a brave is born who will see himself in the eye of the great bear. Back in the old days, sometimes young guys would go out and try to get close to a grizzly—you know—just to prove how brave they were. Grandfather says they usually ended up as bear food. He says the 'Great Spirit' gives the brave as a gift. He determines who it will be, before he is ever born, and only he can speak with the great bear or look into his eyes. I always thought it was just legend—just talk—until today."

"You weren't trying to prove you were brave, were you Bailey? Bailey?"

I kind of jerked. Daddy's eyes studied me for a time. I shook my head.

"No, sir. There . . . well . . . there just wasn't anything else I could do. He was gonna get Kimmerly. And I . . . well . . . I didn't think that was right."

"You're just darned lucky you didn't get ripped to shreds," said the other man who I didn't recognize.

I nodded again. "Yes, sir. I know that."

"The good Lord was sure with you today," Austin put in.

"Maybe the Great Spirit," Grady teased.

"Just pure, blessed luck." Mr. Haskill took another drink of his coffee.

Daddy's smile was gentle.

"Maybe all three," he whispered.

I cleared my throat and got up from the rocker. It was Daddy's favorite chair—the one he always sat in—and I had no idea how I ended up in it.

"Excuse me a minute. I got to go to the outhouse."

I trotted through the front door, around the porch, and to the little house out back. Well, I didn't trot. About every three steps or so, I'd stop, listen, and look all around to make sure there wasn't a bear lurking in the trees. When I got to the outhouse, I sat down on the wood bench between the two holes and buried my face in my hands. All I could do was cry and cry and cry until the sleeves of my shirt were wet. I cried so much, I made myself sick to my stomach. I slipped out the door and went around back. I threw up until I thought my toenails were gonna come out my throat. On the way back to the house, I stopped by the pump, washed my face, and got a drink. It made me feel better.

It was nearly dark before Mr. Haskill and the other two men left. On the way out the door he told me that Daddy had tried to get to me. He said that he and Grady tackled him and wrestled him to the ground, on account of how I had the grizzly stopped dead in his tracks. They were afraid that if they hadn't stopped him, the bear would have torn up both of us.

After they left, Grady and Austin headed back to their room in the barn. We all followed them out on the porch to say good night. At the bottom of the steps Grady stopped and turned to us. Like always, his smile made me feel good when he focused on me.

"Bailey, I know you're kind of quiet and shy. But word of this is gonna get out. Old man Haskill can't keep his mouth shut . . ." Grady kind of broke off what he was saying. He gave a big shrug. "Shoot, not just him. I can't keep my mouth shut about this, neither. I got to tell somebody—especially my grandfather. But my point is that by tomorrow, the story about what happened today will be clean up and down the valley. There will be people showing up. Lots of them. Probably a lot of Flathead—you know, from my tribe. They won't hurt you or bother you. Nothing like that. And Mrs. Trumbull"—he smiled, glancing to her—"there's no need to fix coffee or even make conversation, if you don't want to. They'll just want to look. And, Bailey, you don't need to do nothing, neither. Don't have to say anything. Don't even have to wave. They just want to look at you, then they'll be on their way."

I nodded, letting him know that I understood and that I appreciated him warning me before folks started showing up.

Grady was right. Over the next couple of weeks probably three-fourths of the folks in the whole Flathead Valley showed up at our place. Even people from around Polson, down to the far end of the lake, came.

It was hard to tell the Flathead Indians from anybody else. Except for a few of the older ones, they all wore Levi's or overalls or dresses—just like the rest of us.

We were working on the roof of the barn when Grady's grandfather came. I thought the old man was going to cry when I climbed down off the roof and shook his hand. His old, weathered face stretched to such a smile Grady and me both were afraid it was gonna crack. I didn't much care for all the fuss or attention. Then, I figured if seeing me gave the other folks just half as much happiness as it had Grady's grandfather . . . well, it was worth it.

Over that two weeks Kimmerly would wake up, crying in the nights. My room was right across the hall from hers. I'd go sit on the edge of her bed and pat her shoulder or rub her back until she fell asleep again.

During that two weeks I woke up a couple of times, too. I didn't cry. But I was dripping wet with the cold sweats. Sometimes it was right hard to get back to sleep.

We finally got to go on our fishing trip. We didn't go to the high country around Mr. MacDonald's lake or up to see the glaciers. Daddy took us to the Flathead River. We camped at the park beside the courthouse—right in the middle of Kalispell. Guess Daddy didn't want to run the risk of seeing another bear for a while. That was fine with me. My biggest hope in life was that I'd never, ever see another grizzly bear as long as I lived.

Even in the middle of town we had fun fishing, anyhow.

School started in September. Nobody gave me any problems. Even the redheaded kid in bib overalls wanted to be my friend and hang around with me.

But somehow I knew that he wouldn't stay a friend for very long. I knew that, sooner or later, the bear would be forgotten. Probably by next Fourth of July, somebody would pitch a firecracker too close to me and I'd take off—just like always.

But even as I thought about it, it didn't seem to bother me. I wasn't afraid of being afraid. Not any-more.

Even to this day—sometimes at night when I close my eyes to go to sleep—I can still see that little twelve-year-old boy. At times I think I know him. Other times, I'm not so sure. Really-n-truly, he's nothing special. He's not too smart, but he's not too dumb, either. He's not too brave, but by no means is he a coward. He's just ordinary people. He laughs and eats and all the things that everybody else does. He gets confused and he worries about dumb stuff that he ought not worry about. He's got a good sense of humor and likes to laugh, but sometimes he loses his temper. When that happens, the way he acts em-barrasses him.

Lots of times, he even gets scared. He doesn't like

it. Nobody likes being scared. But it happens—and it's okay. But he doesn't understand why it's okay.

The thing I do know is that he won't ever leave me. That twelve-year-old boy will always be with me. In that twilight time, when sleep draws near, I can still see him in the eye of the great bear.

# About the Author

Since BILL WALLACE's best-selling first novel, *A Dog Called Kitty,* was published in 1980, he has won nineteen state awards for his children's books.

After seven years as a classroom teacher and ten years as the principal and physical education teacher at West Elementary School, which he attended as a child, Wallace is now a full-time author and public speaker. Bill says that although it has been a while since he taught school, he still writes books for his fourth graders—"It's like they're in my head and heart whenever I sit down to work on a story."

He received his M.S. in Elementary Administration from Southwestern State University and studied professional writing with William Foster-Harris and Dwight V. Swain at the University of Oklahoma.

Don't miss these books by

CAROL WALLACE AND BILL WALLACE

## THE FLYING FLEA, CALLIE, AND ME

Callie was getting too old for the job, so the house people picked me to be a mouser. But I didn't plan on getting dive-bombed by a mockingbird building her nest...or adopting the baby who fell out. No joke! Flea—that's what I named her—couldn't even fly. She was pathetic. I had to help her. The first step was protecting Flea—and me—from the monster rats in the barn and Bullsnake under the woodpile. Next, Callie and I had to teach Flea to fly. After all, how could she stay up North with us when her bird family was flying to Florida? I know I'll miss my Flea. But she'll come back—after she's seen the world!

## THAT FURBALL PUPPY AND ME

Here I am, a self-respecting kitten just trying to survive in a rat-eat-cat world, when the humans in my life start acting crazy. Something about the kids, and grandkids, coming to visit for Christmas. Mama accusing me of tearing up the presents. Noisy voices and grabby little hands. If the grandkids are bad, they're nothing compared to the gift the kids gave Mama for Christmas...a puppy! Dumb furball. Everybody is cooing over this yappy puppy who only wants to play. So I got him in trouble for tearing up the kitchen. Big deal. Problem is, I feel responsible. This puppy's headed for T*R*O*U*B*L*E. How can I save him? I can't even save myself!

2413

A MINSTREL® BOOK

Published by Pocket Books

2306-0

Don't Miss These Fun Animal Adventures from

# BILL WALLACE

## UPCHUCK AND THE ROTTEN WILLY

Cats and dogs just can't be friends—or can they?

Iowa Children's Choice Award Master List 2000-2001
Indian Paintbrush Award Master List 1999-2000
Nevada Young Readers Award Master List 1999-2000

## UPCHUCK AND THE ROTTEN WILLY: THE GREAT ESCAPE

It's a dog's life—as told by a cat.

## UPCHUCK AND THE ROTTEN WILLY: RUNNING WILD

It's not so bad living a dog's life. Unless you're a cat.

# Get ready for adventure, mystery, and excitement!

*Nightmare Mountain*

*Sisters, Long Ago*

*Cages*

*Terror at the Zoo*

*Horror at the Haunted House*

*Night of Fear*

*The Richest Kids in Town*

*Deadly Stranger*

*The Volcano Disaster*

*The Blizzard Disaster*

*The Flood Disaster*

*The Secret Journey*

## By Peg Kehret

**Available from Minstrel® Books**
**Published by Pocket Books**

668-14

# Todd Strasser's
# AGAINST THE ODDS™

## Shark Bite
The sailboat is sinking, and Ian just saw the biggest shark of his life.

## Grizzly Attack
They're trapped in the Alaskan wilderness with no way out.

## Buzzard's Feast
Danger in the desert!

## Gator Prey
They know the gators are coming for them...it's only a matter of time.

Published by Pocket Books

2023

## BRUCE COVILLE'S

The fascinating and hilarious adventures of the world's first purple sixth grader!

**I WAS A SIXTH GRADE ALIEN**

**THE ATTACK OF THE TWO-INCH TEACHER**

**I LOST MY GRANDFATHER'S BRAIN**

**PEANUT BUTTER LOVERBOY**

**ZOMBIES OF THE SCIENCE FAIR**

**DON'T FRY MY VEEBLAX!**

**TOO MANY ALIENS**

**SNATCHED FROM EARTH**

**THERE'S AN ALIEN IN MY BACKPACK**

**by Bruce Coville**

A MINSTREL® BOOK

Published by Pocket Books

2304-04